IVORY

Book Three in the Addison-Ross Saga

By KJ Newman

ALICE

"He said what?" Anna's shriek was so shrill that she stopped the Hyde Park boot camp dead. They all turned to look at us and gained a glare from Anna for their trouble. "Seriously, he said that?"

"Yes." My lower lip wobbled, and the stream of tears began again. "He said, 'it was always you.'"

"Who was always you?" Xander asked, collapsing onto the grass, looking dishevelled and hungover, with an unlit cigarette sticking to his lower lip. He tugged it away and licked his lips. "Man, I feel like shit." Xander rummaged in his jacket pocket and produced a lighter, igniting the end of his cigarette and inhaling deeply. "So, what's the big emergency? I'm dying here."

"Lucien is an arsehole."

"Again?"

"He's just pledged undying love to his wife, so yes a huge arsehole!" Anna said sharply. "Why do you think we're here at this ungodly hour on a Saturday? Partying?"

"I just rocked up, Anna. No need to shout. I have a hangover..."

"I don't much care, Xander." Anna almost spat at Xander. "Your hangover will have to wait."

"Don't start with each other!" I whimpered, so pathetically it was embarrassing, and wiped my nose on my sleeve. "I'm sorry I dragged you both here, practically in the middle of the night, but you are my best friends and I had no one else to call and there was no train up to Lucy's in Edinburgh otherwise I would have been on it."

"Looking like that?" Xander asked gesturing. "You look worse than me!"

"Her heart is broken, you unsupportive arse..."

"I am supportive! I'm here, aren't I?"

"Sadly, yes, you are. Have you even been to bed?"

"Not unless you count falling asleep on Hugo's best friend's marble steps."

"You're such a dick!"

"I know!" Xander grinned, "but despite loving conversations revolving around me, Anna dearest, we're here for Alice. Tell me all, sweetie."

2

In between shuddering breaths and a deluge of tears, I told Xander the conversation I'd overheard at Lucien's. To retell it brought fresh heartache and the wound in my chest that had sealed up recently, gaped wide open as I spoke. "I'm so stupid. So stupid. I believed him. I believed in his grand gesture of following me to St Lucia, I believed it was me that he wanted but he no more wanted me than I wanted to share space with the massive spider I found in the shower this morning." I took a painful breath in. "I should never have believed him. I should have stuck with Zac, he liked me, he would have treated me well, instead I shit all over him which makes me just as much of an arsehole as Lucien is."

Zac's kind, handsome face flashed before my eyes. I really screwed that up. All for Lucien. All for a man who could tell his wife that it had always been her. Nausea twisted in my stomach and I leaned over the grass to retch. Anna rubbed my back and made sympathetic cooing noises. Xander looked grossed out.

"You're not an arsehole." Anna said, kicking Xander with an outstretched leg. "You can't help who you fall in love with, it's not a plan that we have any control over. If you had stuck it out with Zac, you really would have been an arsehole because it would have been false. He would have felt more than you and that would have been really unfair."

"I did like Zac…"

"*Like* isn't enough Alice. Like is for a fuck buddy, not for someone who has real feelings for you. You can't spend your life with someone you just *like*, that would be failing…"

"I am failing, Anna. I have failed."

"No, you haven't, you've just fallen for the wrong man. Lucien is practically your first love, there has barely been anyone before him. The first love never works out! The first love is there to give a person something amazing, but it can't last, because that kind of spark doesn't go on forever…"

"There speaks someone who clearly isn't getting any…" Xander said, lying back on the grass.

"Fuck off Xan." Anna said stroppily. "I am actually getting more than I've ever had, not that I need to justify anything to you."

Xander grinned. "But you do, every single time! You are the easiest person in the world to wind up."

"Look," I said standing up and brushing my hair out of my tear-soaked eyes. "Thanks for coming out here to meet me, I'm sorry that it was so early, and I'm really grateful that you love me enough to drag yourself out on a Saturday morning, but I'm going to go home. I can't sit here listening to you two arguing. Normally, yes. Today, no. I need…" I sighed deeply. "I need to be wrapped up in a huge hug and for someone to tell me that shit happens, but that regardless of the shit, I'll be ok, that my heart will mend and one day none of this will be important." My face crumpled and tears fell again. "Because, it doesn't feel like I will ever be ok. I thought it was all going to be perfect. I thought he felt like me, well not exactly like me, but near enough and now it feels like my heart has been ripped from my chest…" I shook my head. *Oh, Isabelle, it was always you.* "I'm so gullible."

"Sorry Alice." Xander said throwing his cigarette onto the grass and jumping up to give me a smoky hug. "I'm sorry Anna and I are being unsupportive dicks, we are here for you, we're always here for you. Don't go home, not like this. Are you sure you heard what you thought you heard?"

"Of course she did," Anna snapped. I wondered if she was having a bad time too and trying to hide it from me. "She wouldn't be here if she had heard something different."

"Just asking." Xander said, pulling me in tighter. "What's with grumpy bollocks?" He whispered in my ear. I shrugged against his slim frame and he squeezed me a little tighter. "Shall we go to the pub? I, for one, could do with a hair of the dog, I feel shit."

"I think you'd be lucky to find one open." I sniffed and pulled away. "Thanks for the lovely hug Xan, but seriously you smell as though you were vomited up by a park bench alcoholic.

Xander raised his arm and inhaled. "Yeah, I do. Gross aren't I?

"Extremely." I stuffed my fists into my eyes as a wave of pain ripped through my centre. "Oh God," I said, crumpling into Xander as my knees gave way. I was in a living, waking nightmare. After everything my association with Lucien had put me through, I'd believed him, believed that he had changed, that he wanted me. He told me his deepest secrets, brought the demons to meet me and I'd walked the painful path with him, only for Isabelle to come back and take what had always been hers.

I killed my daughter.

I hadn't believed that. Lucien didn't lose control, he wasn't the sort of man who ever handed himself over to anyone, never mind drive his young children after he'd been drinking. I was so sure he'd got it wrong. Now, I had no idea of who he was. I didn't know him at all.

It was entirely possible that he had done exactly what he said he had and that I had been completely blind.

"About that drink," I said.

LUCIEN

Isabelle said nothing. The apartment was silent, not even the clock on the wall ticked. *Do you still love me Lucien?* It had always been her. From the moment I saw her, I'd fallen hard, and she'd wrapped herself around my heart and stopped it beating for anyone else.

Of course, she'd walked out on me after the crash that killed our daughter, the crash she had blamed me for. Isabelle had left me fighting for my life in a hospital bed, scooped up our five-year-old daughter, Henrietta, and disappeared. I'd seen Isabelle once in a decade, when she arrived unexpectedly last year and hurled such venom at me, that I nearly died. Had it not been for Alice, I would have.

Alice was my guardian angel but each second that Isabelle was here in my apartment, jeopardised my relationship with her. Alice would arrive any moment, filled with an uncontrollable heat from the promises I'd made. A heat that, until Isabelle turned up unannounced, I had been burning from.

Shit.

"You have to go." I said eventually, lifting my head from my hands and staring at my wife. I wanted to see the girl that she used to be, but there was nothing in the thin, pinched, angry woman in front of me that I recognised.

"What do you mean, it was always me?" She asked softly, standing up and straightening her pencil skirt in the way that always used to turn me on. Slow, deliberate movements, palms flat against the material, smoothing it down over her flat stomach and slim hips.

"Please go, Isabelle."

"Tell me, Lucien."

"Tell me where Hettie is."

"I've already told you that she doesn't want to see you. It has taken ten years for her to stop screaming in the night…"

"I'm still screaming, Isabelle." I interrupted her as Hettie's lovely, five-year-old face came in front of my eyes. Isabelle stood before me, hands on her hips, her face twisted in what I can only imagine she thought to be an understanding face.

"I'm sure you do, Lucien. None of us will recover from losing Ottie, not me, not Hettie and not you. It was a tragic mistake, a mistake that should never have happened."

"Was it really my fault?" I asked feeling the searing pain in my stomach. "Was I drunk, Isabelle?"

She nodded slowly.

"Why did you let me drive?"

"I don't know." Isabelle whispered, her lower lip quivering. "If I could turn back time…"

"I know." I said quietly. "That longing never goes away, does it."

"Do you still love me Lucien?" Isabelle asked again, her voice was barely audible when she spoke. "You said it was always me, what does that mean?"

I looked as her face changed into a myriad of expressions, none I could read apart from one. Confusion. I blew out a long breath and said, "it was always you, Isabelle. Always. From the moment I saw you in that bar in Manchester, wearing that tiny gold dress, you completely blew me away. I never believed I could want someone so much, to have such a fierce desire for someone that it took my breath away. I thought it would last forever…" I raked my hands through my hair and momentarily closed my eyes. "But it all went wrong, didn't it? I wasn't enough for you. What I gave you wasn't enough, and I lost us trying to make you happy. I loved you for years, Isabelle, through the years when you loved me back, and for all those years that followed when you hated me, I still loved you."

"And now?" She asked fixing her gaze on mine.

"Now? Now I love someone else."

"Your brunette?"

"Yes. My brunette, my guardian angel…Her name is Alice"

"Alice?" Isabelle rolled the name around her tongue. "Alice…such a sweet name, but I wonder, does this guardian angel know what you did?" Isabelle said, her voice low and threatening. I know what she wanted, she wanted a hold over me, but this time she wasn't going to get it. "Does she know you killed your child?"

"Yes." I replied simply.

Isabelle looked surprised, then her face reddened with anger. "And she's ok with that? Your guardian angel is ok with you killing your beautiful innocent little girl?"

I wasn't rising to her bait. Isabelle wanted me to flip, to have some reason to walk out the door and use my anger to keep Hettie from me, probably forever. I don't believe that she would ever let me back into Hettie's life. She was going to make me pay for what I did, with my blood or my sanity, or, if she stayed much longer, with my relationship with Alice. "She's ok with me being me."

Isabelle's mouth gapped open as her mind wrapped itself around my words. It was clear she had been hoping for a different answer, one she could use against me, as she had used everything else in our last painful meeting. Eventually she said, "sign the papers Lucien."

"I've already said, you can have a divorce, Isabelle, you can have whatever the fuck you want, but Jean-Claude is not adopting Hettie."

"How many times do I have to tell you, that it is what she wants, not me?"

"And how many times do I have to tell you, she needs to tell me herself." I reached across the coffee table for the brown envelope that Isabelle had flung at me and opened it. There were two legal documents contained within in it, the adoption documents I pushed to one side, but I took my time reading the divorce papers.

"You're not asking for a settlement?"

"No."

"Why?"

"I don't want your money, Lucien."

"I have money for Hettie…"

"What makes you think she wants your money?"

"I'll keep it for when I see her." I said, not wanting to get into another argument. I kept glancing at the clock. Shit, Alice was due any moment and the last thing I wanted was for her to find Isabelle in all her scathing glory in my apartment. "What have you done for money?"

"I had some."

"From where?"

"It doesn't matter."

"Jean-Claude?"

"No."

"Me? Did you take it from me?"

Isabelle shrugged. "I took what I needed."

"My daughter, my heart and my money! I surprised you stopped there."

Isabelle made a grab for the papers. "I could take the lot." She snapped.

"Take it. I don't care. Money doesn't make anyone happy, despite what I thought growing up."

"It's not money though, is it Lucien, it's whiskey and women, just like your dad."

"Don't be a bitch, Isabelle. I could just as easily drag up your sorry past, so keep a lid on what you say."

We sat in silence as I read the documents. No hidden clauses, no surprises. "I don't agree with sole custody of Henrietta, have your lawyer change that and then I'll sign it." I stuffed the papers back into the envelope and threw it back on the table.

"I won't."

"Then I won't sign," I told her, "and we'll have reached an impasse and you won't be able to marry Jean-Claude."

"Bastard."

"I have never pretended to be anything else Isabelle." I leaned back on the sofa and folded my arms above my head. "Shut the door on your way out. I don't want you here when Alice gets here."

"Perhaps we should be introduced."

"Perhaps you should just leave, Isabelle.

She snatched up the envelope. "Don't make an enemy of me, Lucien."

"What else can you possibly do to me, that you haven't already done? There is nothing left to threaten me with."

"Isn't there?" She said, turning on her heel and walking towards the door. "It may not suit you to find out."

The force of the door slamming knocked a picture off the wall. Somehow, whatever it took, I would find Hettie. Even if it was the last thing I did, I would find her.

ALICE

Xander had predictably found the dingiest bar in all of London. We were somewhere near Marble Arch, in a bar that smelt of stale tobacco and vomit. I'd lost track of the time, merely counting the number of pints the alcoholic with a nose like a potato, swaying next to me, had consumed. It was impressive. In a sad-as-fuck kind of way, but I feared I was matching him with the glasses of cheap, vinegary wine that I kept reaching for.

I should not have been given alcohol. It seemed like a good idea at the time, filling the void inside me with wine, but the wine was nasty and all I had was a vile, bitter taste in my mouth.

Anna was beyond help. She was drunker than I was, having had a blazing row with Toby, probably because she was as pissed as a fart before midday when she should have been somewhere with him. She was leaning over the bar, her face twisted into what she probably thought was a seductive look, pressing her breasts together with her arms at the balding, sweaty bartender who looked as though all his Christmases had come at once. At any moment he was going to dive head-first into her cleavage and drown.

I knew we should go. This had been a terrible idea and Anna was in serious danger of doing something she would never forgive herself for. If I had to listen to her telling Sweaty that he looked just like Hugh Jackman one more time I would vomit on the floor. I reached for my glass but thought better of it and, peeling my feet from the sticky floor, I crossed the room to wake Xander, who was snoring on one of the revolting torn sofas in the corner.

"Xan?" I slurred, reaching uncoordinatedly for him, "Xan?"

He grunted and turned over, knocking his pint to the floor. It shattered on the painted wood and the bartender looked over with undisguised annoyance. He didn't rush to clear it up, though, instead took his time pouring out a cider for potato nose and topping up his shot glass with whiskey.

It must be an easy path to alcoholism, I thought to myself as I tried to wake Xander. So easy. I ran my tongue around my furry teeth and grimaced. Yuck, perhaps not that easy. "Xander." I said more forcefully, "we need to go before Anna ends up in the toilet with the bartender."

"Wha…wha…what? Anna? Where?" Xander sat up blearily and wiped the drool from his chin. "She's over there…"

"I know!"

"You made it seem as if she'd been kidnapped. Urgh, I feel like shit."

"You look like shit."

"Says you!" Xander said, squinting at me through red rimmed eyes. "How drunk are you? You're swaying, it's like being sea-sick." He went a funny shade of green. "Stop moving."

"I can't help it. I'm drunk. Drunker than I should be. Xan do you think I could be an alcoholic?"

"Nah, you're not desperate enough. Well, not yet anyway. Fuck, my head hurts. What time is it?" He asked, struggling to get his phone from his pocket. "Shit, I've got a million missed calls from Hugo. He has no idea where I am, I said I was coming to your rescue and that I wouldn't be long…"

"Some rescue!" The nausea was coming over me like a tidal wave. "Xan, I feel really sick."

"Alice?" My heart sank to my toes. "Alice, what the fuck are you doing in here?"

Lucien. The God, the Devil, the Finder of Broken-Hearted Drunk People had somehow found me. He'd often turned up, unexpectedly, to random places I had been, with no explanation of how he knew. Once I'd asked him if he was the devil, but now I knew he was more than that.

"What the fuck do you want Lucien?" I said, shaking my head as I spoke in a whisper, keeping my back to him so he couldn't see the pain on my face. *Hold it together, Alice, hold it together.* "Haven't you done enough?" I squeezed my eyes tightly together and felt suddenly, horribly, sober. There was a throbbing in my head as the pain in my chest worsened. "I must have been mad to trust you." My upset exploded out of me and I felt a rush of anger. "So, it was always Isabelle? Of course, it was! How could I have ever believed anything different? Silly, dumb Alice. Please go the fuck away Lucien." My arms instinctively wrapped around my middle, holding me together and the rage subsided. "I can't believe I'm back here again."

"What the fuck…No, Alice, you've got it all wrong, always you jump to conclusions." He said crossly. I heard his tread on the sticky floor as he moved two steps closer to me. Xander flicked his eyes between Lucien and I, then stood up and, squeezing my hand, he crossed the room towards Anna.

"Do I?"

"Every time. Always you look for excuses." Lucien took a few more steps towards me until I could feel the heat from his body on my back and smell the citrus scent of him that was like a drug to me. "It's not about Isabelle…"

"I heard you." My voice broke and I coughed. "I heard her ask you if you still loved her and you said, 'it was always you.' I heard all of it, Lucien."

"Is that why I found you in this shit hole? Because you heard that?"

"Yes." I sniffed. "It was the only bar open."

"It's a hell hole."

"Yeah, well when a person feels like hell, a hole opens up."

Lucien sighed behind me. "I'm not having a conversation with your back in a grotesque bar that smells of piss and bad beer."

"How did you even find me?"

"I have my ways, Alice."

"You're as creepy as fuck, Lucien." I turned on my heel and stomped across the bar. Anna was being encouraged down from the bar stool by Xander who was receiving daggers from the bar tender. I couldn't blame the man for thinking he was in with Anna, her breasts had spent the entire time pointing in his direction, sadly for him, he was out of luck and I heard Xander speaking to Toby on her phone, whilst helping her down from the stool.

"I can manage, Xander." She snapped, falling into a heap on the floor as he let her go."

"Get up Anna, you'll catch something down there." Xander hauled her to her feet and marched her from the bar. "Toby is coming for you and I'm going home to beg Hugo's forgiveness."

"Is that Lucien?" Anna squinted up from the floor. "How did he find you in here?" Her face took on an expression that was a drunk, uncoordinated version of her usual impressed face. "I hope you're not going to go all sappy and forgive him." She poked her tongue out at Lucien and then gave into a fit of giggles. "I'm so drunk."

"Come on, Anna." Lucien pushed past me to hoist Anna up from the floor. "My car is outside. I'll take you home. Xander, tell Toby I've got her."

"You're so masterful, Lucien." Anna said leaning against him. "Alice is a lucky girl. Oh no," she clamped her hand over her mouth, "I forgot, you're a wife-loving arsehole."

"Am I?" He replied grimly flashing me a pissed-off look. "Interesting."

Lucien half dragged, half guided Anna from the bar. Xander took my hand and we followed them out. I was feeling nauseous. The bad wine and early drinking were taking a toll on me and I longed to lie down in a cool, dark room and sleep it off. I wondered if I was playing the romance game all wrong. Even after all the months with Lucien, I was still unsure of him, still unsure of how to manage my feelings for him. His conversation with Isabelle had shaken me to the very core but I was confused – was he here to tell me it was over or was he here to tell me I had gotten things very wrong?

His face was grim as he bent Anna into the car. She leaned against the door and pressed the button to wind down the window. "Sorry Alice, I was supposed to be there for you, instead I got drunk and now your arsehole boyfriend is taking me home."

"Get in, Alice." Lucien said, sharply. He looked over at Xander who was swaying. "Do you need a lift?"

"No, man, Hugo is coming." Lucien nodded at Xander curtly. Xander returned the gesture with a beaming grin and wrapped me in a tight hug. "He's here, Alice," he whispered. "It can't be what you thought."

"He's probably here to tell me he's running off into the sunset with her."

"Nah, not with that cross look on his face!" Xander gave me a loud, smacking kiss on the cheek. "I'm going to meet my beloved so he can take me home and put me to bed. Not convinced it will be my preferred afternoon in bed, I suspect I won't be able to get it up. I'm broken!" Xander burped loudly. "Fuck me, that was bad beer. I'll ring you tomorrow." He turned from me to Anna. She was snoring, her mouth hanging open and her head leaning against the door frame. Lucien pushed her head onto the rest and wound the window up. He didn't look impressed.

"He looks really hot when he's mad." Xander commented. He checked an incoming message and grinned. "My knight in a shining Aston Martin is around the corner. Love you." I watched him wobble along the road and turn left onto Piccadilly. Lucien slammed the car door and began impatiently revving the engine. I didn't know what to do – get in with him and wait for whatever he had to say or run away.

The impatient revving continued and with a sigh, and a feeling of impending doom, I got into the back of the car.

LUCIEN

Taking a pissed-up dribbling mess to north London wasn't part of my Saturday plan but as I handed Anna over to her boyfriend, I did have a rather peculiar sense of gratitude to her and Xander for looking after Alice. Alice may have ended up in a shit-hole that smelt as though it was frequented permanently by London's great unwashed, but her friends had dropped everything for her, and I had begrudgingly given them my mentally-offered thanks, although hell would freeze over before I said the words. I was fucked off. I was so fucked off I could have spat acid. There was no escape from the mistakes of the past and until I could find Hettie, there would be no real rest. Having Alice in my life calmed the panic attacks, but until the nightmare was resolved, I feared they were just biding their time before the explosion came. I feared that time. I feared it because losing Alice troubled me and I didn't believe I would survive without her.

I looked in the rear-view mirror. Alice was staring out of the window, leaning her head on her palm, elbow against the door. She looked lost in thought, or, more specifically, just lost. I felt anxiety grip my stomach. Fucking Isabelle. Fucking…me.

Isabelle and her demands had thrown arctic water all over the raging horn that I'd woken up with and now Alice stank of cheap alcohol and looked as though she was likely to throw up at any moment.

It was my fault that she and her friends had ended up in an incoherent mess but whether Alice would believe what I would say, I was unsure. I often felt that she was waiting for me to trip up so that she could believe what her version of our truth was. Alice was mistrusting of me still, and if she'd half heard the conversation I'd had with Isabelle, it was going to take a lot more than my charm to make her feel secure.

Shit, my demons would never let me be free. They held on so tightly that some days, like today, they doused my life with flammable liquid and threw a burning rag onto it.

"You alright?" I asked. My voice sounded loud in the silence car and Alice jumped.

"Fabulous." She replied flatly.

"Do you want some water?" I held up the plastic bottle beside me in the cup holder.

"Yes please." Alice leaned forward and took it hesitantly from me, unscrewing the lid and raising it to her lips. She drank most of it. "How did you find me?"

"I have my ways."

"So, you say."

I sighed and clenched the steering wheel. The car was not the place for the conversation that was coming. "Are you hungry?"

"Why?"

"It didn't look like the sort of establishment that sold food."

"It wasn't."

"Alice…"

"Don't! Don't say anything, Lucien. Don't give me any bullshit, don't tell me I'm a great girl but, blah, blah, blah. You don't need to say anything, I heard you."

"Yes, you said that."

"You don't deny it."

"No."

"Then," she said, taking a shuddering breath in. "There is nothing else to say. Goodbye Lucien." The car was stopped at red lights as Alice released the seatbelt and clambered from the car. I could do nothing as she slammed the door and ran off along the road.

"Shit. Fucking shit. SHIT." I pounded the steering wheel with my fists with nowhere to go but forward with the traffic.

Countless scenarios fought for space in my head as I crawled along the north circular, until a sheen of sweat marred my brow. Hettie. Isabelle. Alice. Jean-Claude.

Jean-fucking-Claude. My best friend. The man who saved my life after the crash, the man who falsified my hospital records to eradicate the alcohol that was in my blood, the one who said Ottie was a terrible, dreadful accident that couldn't have been avoided – that same man was taking my child from me. *Jean-Claude is her father now.* Jean-Claude? Was he the answer?

I dialled a number on my mobile and a gruff voice answered.

"John?"

16

"Lucien?"

"I need you to find Jean-Claude Benoit. I think he holds the key."

"On it." The phone went dead. I reset the sat-nav and drove towards Alice's flat.

ALICE

My head pounded. Sobering up on a stuffy Saturday afternoon was a new kind of hell. I'd lay on the sofa alternating between bawling and heaving until I felt exhausted and wretched. The day had started out so promising, the lure of Lucien and his new array of toys had me floating across London on a wave of searing heat, my insides slowly flowing out of me. My panties were soaked by the time I'd reached Lucien's front door, my pussy quivering with the pent-up excitement of knowing I would be at his decadent mercy, until I heard her. *Do you still love me Lucien?*

I wanted him to say no, to say that it was only me, that she was now a distant memory from a past long buried. But he didn't. *Oh, Isabelle, it was always you.* I didn't have the streetwise experience of dealing with someone like him, the games, the control – I wasn't from a life like that, he was the first one. He was the one I'd fallen for so completely that I was always uncertain about him. I loved him too much to ever feel secure. Perhaps it was for the best that I knew now. I was only twenty-eight. There was time to meet someone new, time to fall in love with someone with whom forever was a possibility, or if not in love, at least like well enough that it would be ok.

I'd questioned myself over and over – was it over, did he come to find me to explain or did he come to find me to leave me? I didn't know how to play this game. Lucien was worldly wise, sharp, clever, a multimillionaire who'd survived the cutthroat world of business, despite his personal life falling apart. I was none of those things. He overwhelmed me most of the time. That could surely not be a basis for a long-lasting relationship? I'd always believed that relationships were built on mutual everything, healthy ones anyway. Had I been in an unhealthy relationship with Lucien? Was I still an agreement, despite his protestations to the contrary?

Was it still Isabelle?

I was going to send myself insane with the unending analysis of my relationship with Lucien, but I felt too ropey to do anything but lie on the sofa feeling bereft. Anna had text to check up on me, but she was equally as hungover and feeling mortified that she had flirted with the barman. *'I told him he looked like Hugh Jackman,'* she messaged, and I could hear her groan across the airwaves. *'I mean, WTF?'*

'We all do crazy things when we're drunk.' I replied.

'I want to die.'

'Please don't!'

I did know how she felt. I'd done plenty of insane things whilst under the influence of alcohol, mainly Lucien related but I did understand her mortification, although I'd done most of my questionable things whilst sober. Lucien was my drug and when I was around him, sense went out of the window.

I rolled myself off the sofa and went to my small bathroom to clean my teeth again. The cheap, nasty wine had left my teeth feeling as though they would crumble from my mouth, but no amount of brushing would freshen the taste. In the end, unable to stand it any longer, I dragged myself to the shop for mouth wash. I should have known Lucien would be on my doorstep when I got back.

He didn't look very happy.

"Lucien." I said, leaning past him to unlock the door. The close proximity to him set off the fizz in my belly and the couple of deep breathes of his citrus scent, made it worse.

"Do you plan to retain this immaturity Alice?" He asked sharply. Fuck, he smelt good. Lucien took a step back from me and I assumed it was because I had the stench of the bar on my skin.

"I'm sorry?" I pulled a face. "Immaturity? Not sure I know what you mean, Lucien."

He went to grab my arm but instead wrinkled his nose and took a step backwards. "You stink."

I shrugged and pushed the door open. "And?"

Lucien took an exasperated breath in. "Don't be petulant, Alice."

"I can be whatever the fuck I choose."

Lucien grabbed my arm and swung me over his shoulder in a fireman's lift. Despite me flailing my spare arm and trying to kick out with my legs, he had me in a firm grip that gave me no chance to escape. I hated my body responding to his action, hated that the pulse deep within me began to beat louder and louder until I was sure he would hear.

"Put me down, Lucien. PUT ME THE FUCK DOWN." Of course, he ignored me as he crossed my flat and took me into the bathroom, dumping me in the bath fully clothed and turning the overhead shower on full. It was freezing. I spluttered and the next moment a liberal dollop of shower gel was squirted over bare areas of skin. "What the fuck are you doing?"

"You stink. I am not having a conversation with you while you smell like the shit tip I found you in."

"I don't want to have a conversation with you full stop. I want you to go away." The water had warmed up, but my dripping clothes were weighing heavily on me which made lifting myself up more complicated, particularly as the bathtub was slippery with shower gel. "Can you get the fuck out of my bathroom." I pulled myself up with the side of the bath and glared at Lucien. "In fact, just get out of my flat. Go back to Isabelle, I don't want you here."

"You're such a liar, Alice." Lucien said, sitting down on the lid of the toilet. "You didn't get in this state because you wanted me to go away."

"No, you're right, I got into this state because you are a head-fucker devil person…"

"I thought you knew me better than that."

"So did I."

"Perhaps you should have just asked me? Instead of running away and getting drunk in a dive bar…"

"Like you've never been drunk in a dive bar?" I snapped, pushing water and hair out of my face. "You seem to have forgotten that fact!"

"For fuck's sake, Alice, I didn't come here to argue with you."

"You should have thought about that before you proclaimed everlasting love for your wife and dumped me in the sodding shower."

"You're sexy when you're angry."

"Fuck off Lucien."

It both annoyed me and turned me on when his mouth turned up into a slow, sexy smile. Fuck, he was hot. Hotter than hot and the longer he looked at me the more hot I became. I must have looked ridiculous, standing, soaking, in the shower covered in shower gel.

"Can you go, please."

"Alice, Alice, Alice…" He said lightly, shaking his head and tutting. "You are like a broken record. I've heard this so many times and you no more mean it today, than you did the other million times."

"You're such an egotist, Lucien."

"Yes, I know, it's all part of my charm!"

"Why did you come here, Lucien? To rub my face in things, to humiliate me, to tell that you're riding of into the sunset with your precious Isabelle…"

"Always so quick to believe the worst of me, aren't you?" He snarled. "Such a silly little girl at times."

"I am not a silly little girl, you patronising arsehole. I heard you. I heard what you said…"

"No, you didn't. You heard some of it, had you bothered to wait and eavesdrop a little longer, you would not have ended up smelling like a pissed-up hobo in a dump."

"Go home, Lucien."

"No. You get washed, I'll wait outside, then we'll speak like grown-ups. Unless you need help washing." There was a twinkle in his eyes when he spoke. A twinkle that went straight to my pussy and melted it. Where Lucien was concerned my resolve just dissolved. I wanted to stand up to him, to be his equal but I was so unsure of him, of us, that it gave him the upper hand. I know what I had heard, and I was certain that Isabelle had him in her grip, but he was here, and it confused me. I waited until he left the room then, wearily, I stripped off my clothes and massaged the shower gel into my skin. I took my time. I had no intention of giving Lucien any more power than he already had. I was bloody well going to stay in the shower until the hot water ran out.

I did not expect Lucien to come crashing through the door and climb into the bath to kiss me with such ferocity that my knees buckled beneath me.

I may have been as mad as hell but fuck me, the man knew how to kiss.

21

LUCIEN

Alice had been deliberately making me wait and the more the minutes ticked by, the more annoyed I'd felt. It was probably wrong of me, I'm not sure I would have reacted any differently if Zac Eaton had asked her a similar question to the one Isabelle asked me, but the entire day had been shat on and it didn't help my mood.

I'd had so much planned, mainly involving Alice being naked, on her knees, and very, very willing to play. Her love of play had increased since our relationship had changed. It had been on her terms, not mine, I was guided by her needs, and while most of the time our hot, frenetic sex was what you may call 'vanilla', there were times when she made it very clear what she wanted, and I was not one to resist.

I paced the small space in the room. I loved Alice's messy, cluttered flat with the cheap prints up on the walls and the colourful throws over the sofa, but I preferred the ordered calm of my apartment. I wondered often how our two personalities would mix. Alice spent most nights at mine, but we hadn't yet had the 'moving in' conversation, and until today's mess was sorted out, that conversation was not imminent.

It had been easier to keep myself locked away from feeling anything for anyone, instead keeping a variety of women for playtime. Alice had crashed into my life and turned my very controlled existence upside down, and now she was upset and angry. They say eavesdroppers never hear well of themselves, in this case, Alice had missed the part of the conversation that would have prevented this situation from happening.

I had told the truth. It had always been Isabelle. Through the good times and the bad times, it had been her although the love turned to bitterness, anger and an obsession that kept me awake at night. It had been good once, greater than good, it had been a fairy tale, if such things existed, but good things don't last and when the death of a child is thrown into the mix, love can turn to hate in a blink of an eye. And now there was Alice.

Good, kind, funny, quirky Alice. Alice who had brought the light back and pushed the demons underground. They stayed away when she was around, but I was uncertain of her. I knew how she felt, she didn't have to say anything, it was obvious, but I also realised that it balanced on a knife edge and we could very easily lose it all.

Like she waited for Isabelle, I waited for Zac. No man, once in love with Alice, would let her go that easily and despite his background making painfully perfect reading, I didn't trust him. I also waited for Alice to realise she'd made a mistake and for her to realise that she wanted someone who had no baggage. Someone like Zac Eaton who served Queen and country like a goddamn hero, not a fucked-up mess like me.

I hated that she still had his number on her phone. I hated that she still worked in the Hub, for now at least, and that his sister was her Girl Friday. I hated that he could just walk in and dazzle her, steal her away from me with a flicker of his baby fucking blues. I hated him because he made me nervous, and nervous was something I'd not been in a decade.

I looked over at the bathroom door. Come on, Alice. The waiting was painful. Knowing that Alice was naked just beyond the door was worse. I wanted her. Like every single moment, of every single day, I wanted her. Alice's soft, ripe body wrapped around mine was the most pleasurable way to spend my time and her being in a mood with me, didn't quell the pull. I readjusted my trousers around my twitching cock. I had to have her, mood, anger, the lot. I'd take it all for a fuck with Alice, hard, fast and fierce. My cock strained against my zipper and I crossed the small room and banged open the bathroom door. Before Alice could complain, I was standing in the bathtub, her hair twisted in my hand pulling her head back so she had no choice but to look at me. There was fire in her eyes when I kissed her. It was a kiss of ownership and belonging, control and surrender, love and anger.

In Alice, I could get lost.

ALICE

I didn't want to want him. I didn't want to wrap my hands in his hair and kiss him with the same need as he kissed me. I didn't want my body to swell against him, nor did I want to feel the hardness of his erection against my stomach. I didn't want to enjoy the tug of my hair wrapped in his fist, I didn't want my pussy to soften and moisten. I wanted to tell him to leave me alone. I wanted to mean it.

"Alice." Lucien groaned against my mouth, his stubble prickling my skin. "Kiss me, Alice."

I pulled him closer to me and kissed him so fiercely that my lips felt bruised. Would I ever tired of this, of the intensity of my feelings, would I ever be able to walk away if I had too? Was he kissing me goodbye, or kissing me to stay? He was soaking wet and the shower had lost its heat but still we kissed, pulling at each other's lips, me ripping the clothes from his body until he was naked before me. His body was strong, firm, godlike, as though he had been sent down from the heavens, or up from the bowels of hell to tempt me with the apple.

Lucien turned me from him, up against the wall and pushed the small of my back until I was bending forward. The tiles were cold against my face, but I knew what was coming and it heated up the inside of me until my skin was burning.

"You still want me to leave?" He asked thickly, gripping my hair tighter than was comfortable. "Do you? Say the word, Alice, say the word."

He was taunting me. Lucien knew what my body was doing whilst being held by him. He knew what I was waiting for, despite my mind screaming 'no'. He knew I wouldn't say the word he'd given me. Red, our word, the safe word, the word he used so glibly in Paris just a few months ago.

I said nothing. Just waited as the heat inside me rose. The water raining down from the shower, was barely lukewarm but it cooled my skin as I leaned against the tiles, palms out to steady myself. The anticipation mounted as Lucien stood behind me deliberating his actions. Then he spanked me. It was short and sharp, the sound reverberated around the small bathroom and I gasped as the sweet pain burned its way around my body. I shouldn't have liked it, shouldn't have desired more and more of it but when Lucien brought out his dominant side, the inner sub in me weakened and I always gave in.

Isabelle was long forgotten as he brought his palm down onto my arse in quick succession. I cried out over and over as my stinging flesh brought a heightened sense of desire that flowed through me, driving out all thoughts of anything other than the craving I had for Lucien. I loved the delinquent side to me, this sexy version of sensible, boring Alice, who accepted the pleasurable pain as a precursor to exquisite, animalistic sex. Lucien knew what my body wanted, what I had been made for and he knew he could make me sing.

Lucien dragged me upwards and back towards the shower. My knees were weak, but his strong arms supported me as he stood me under the cool water, turning up the hot tap to the maximum. Opening the shower gel and squeezing some into his palms, Lucien slowly massaged it into my skin, over my high, swollen breasts, pausing to flick my nipples, and down over my rounded stomach to my pussy.

The heavy ache was unbearable, and I pushed my groin into his hand, urging him to touch me, stroke me, finger-fuck me, anything to take the weight away. I wanted to cum, needed him to make me cum, but Lucien was a man who enjoyed control, and my impatience only made him move more slowly.

"Please." I groaned, moving my hips against him. "Please."

"I thought you wanted me to go?" Lucien whispered, his mouth dusting my ear. "I thought you wanted me to go away?" He pulled his mouth away and stood back, appraising me. I kept my eyes lowered for fear of what I'd see in his eyes. "I wonder, what does little Alice want? Something? Or nothing? Shall I fuck you, or shall I leave you here, wet and wanting? Shall I make you suck my cock, or shall I eat you? Shall I make you beg for it? Beg for me? Beg for a fuck? I'd like that, Alice. I like hearing you beg. It makes me hard, really fucking hard." Lucien leaned over me and took the shower from its holder. He said nothing as he rinsed the shower gel from me. I watched the trail of suds flow into the plug hole.

Lucien twisted the shower head and the water came out forcefully. With a dark look on his face he moved the head between my legs. The water rained upwards like small shards of glass that shattered against my clitoris. It was intense and powerful against my pulsing nub. I closed my eyes and leaned back against the wall. I knew he wouldn't let me orgasm like that, but as the delicious heat began to rise in me, the sounds of my pleasure began to fill the air. Soft moans as my hands moved from the wall to my breasts, huge and swollen with peaked nipples that burned as I touched them. I tugged and pulled at them as the shower water stabbed at my clit, gasping as the sensation spread heat around my body. Everything was forgotten as I let my desire take over.

My groans got louder and the more they did, the harder Lucien's cock got. I longed for it, longed to suck it, feel it, have it inside me, filling me, and he knew it. Drops of pre-cum were glinting at the end, and the longing for him intensified.

"Lucien…"

I couldn't finish my begging. Before I could take a breath, he had me bent over again, one hand twisted in my hair, the other on my hip as he spread my legs and slammed into me.

LUCIEN

My balls ached as they smashed against Alice's arse, my cock buried deep in her. Her pussy was tight around me, the muscles contracting and releasing as I moved in and out of her. Fucking Alice was the best part of the day, even though this fuck was more about control than it was about my release. I had to have her, had to feel her wetness as she climaxed around my cock, because I was still unsure about what was going to happen next.

I'd never fucked anyone who responded like Alice did when I touched her. I'd never fucked anyone who made my body respond like it did when she touched me. I'd had plenty of lovers, plenty of playmates, dominated plenty of willing women but it was different with Alice. It was so primal that I could easily lose control and hand myself over to her. I wanted to. I wanted to give all of me to her, but I feared her rejection and after the events of today, I wasn't sure she would accept it. I could feel her swaying between anger and desire as I fucked her. I wasn't going to last much longer, and from the sounds Alice was making, she was on the edge too.

I pulled out of her and lifted her up into my arms. My mouth found hers as I stepped over the bath and onto the mat. She gripped my hair tightly as she kissed me back, tugging at my lower lip with her teeth. I lay her down on the mat and leaned over her, taking her rosy nipples into my mouth and suckling her. Alice arched her back, pushing her chest up to me and I cupped her breasts, holding them as my mouth pulled at her nipples. She tasted so sweet with a delicate floral scent that drove me wild. I moved backwards, positioning my cock between her swollen breasts and started to slide up and down. She reached under me, taking my balls in her hands and squeezing until I couldn't hold back. My cock fizzed as the bubbles of cum moved below the surface and my cry, as I exploded around her neck, filled the bathroom with an animal sound. The world stopped for a moment as I looked down on her.

Alice had her head back, her eyes closed, and a faint blush covered her face. She didn't look as she did ordinarily, there was no look of pleasure, more an anguish that she was unable to mask. She had given into me, still believing everything she had overheard. She thought this was the last time, I knew her well enough to see the loss in her face.

"Alice?" I whispered, pulling the hand towel down to clean her up. She didn't respond although her eyelids flickered at the touch of the fabric. "Alice, speak to me."

She squeezed her eyes tightly and a lone tear rolled down her cheek.

"I believed you." She said, her voice barely audible. "I thought it was me that you wanted."

"I do want you." I said, taking hold of her hand and putting her palm against my cheek. Alice didn't pull back, but she curled up, hiding her body from me. My handprint on her arse didn't look as sexy now, it looked brutal. She had enjoyed the spanks, her gasps of pleasure were testament to that, but how it now made me feel was a whole new level of self-loathing. Her shame was touchable, and I was mortified. Hurting Alice was never part of my plan, but it seemed that my demons held her to ransom every single time.

"I don't believe you." She said distantly. "I want to believe you but…"

"Believe me." I wrapped her in the bath towel from the rail beside the shower, sensing her nakedness was adding to her shame. She wrapped her arms around it, taking her hand from my cheek to do, and the absence of her warmth suddenly made me fearful.

"Why?"

"Because it's the truth," I said, lying down on the cold floor beside her and wrapping my body around hers. Goosebumps popped up on my arms and torso, and I moved closer to her, close enough that I could feel her heart beating.

"Is it?"

"Yes." I kissed her shoulder and nuzzled into her neck. "It absolutely is."

Alice stiffened beside me. "So why is it so hard to believe?"

"Perhaps you don't want to?"

"I heard you, Lucien."

"Not all of it." I twisted myself and stood up. Alice gripped the bath towel tighter to her. "I can't speak to you lying on the bathroom floor." I held my hand out, but she curled up tighter. "Do I have clothes here?"

"In the cupboard." She said not looking at me.

"Alice…"

"Just give me a minute."

I hesitated for the briefest of moments before I left the bathroom. I walked into Alice's room, stepping over discarded clothing as I took the few short steps to her wardrobe. There was a pair of joggers, a hoodie and a tee-shirt hanging up, remnants from the day she rescued me from a dive bar in Shoreditch. Not my finest hour but it opened my eyes to so much that I had to be thankful for. The reason for my thankfulness was currently lying on her bathroom floor with a wall built around her so high that I wasn't sure I would be able to see over it.

"Shit, shit, shit." I had handled it all wrong. I should have come here to talk, not to kiss her, dominate her, use her…at times I got things so fucking wrong that it was a wonder I could put one foot in front of the other. The door opened and Alice walked in, wrapped in her dressing gown, looking at me warily.

"I'm confused." She said, sitting down on the bed. "You confuse me, you've always confused me. Being around you seems to short-circuit my brain and I don't like it. I don't like feeling like this."

"Like what?"

"Having my insecurities laid out for everyone to see."

"So you got drunk?"

Alice turned her face from me but looked at me from the corner of her eye. "Are you really going there?"

I pulled the joggers up over my thighs. Alice feigned disinterest as I shrugged the t-shirt on, but I took my time pulling it down. She never hid her attraction to me, and my ego enjoyed her desire for my body. I worked hard at it, killer workouts every day to keep myself in shape. I didn't know what I was doing it for, until I met Alice.

"No." I shook my head. Alice wrapped her arms around her waist and glared at me. "Angry?"

"Fuming."

I took a deep breath in and blew it out loudly. "Why this time? Because you overheard half a conversation or because you gave into me again?"

"Don't be an arsehole."

"I'm being an arsehole? I think today, it is you, Alice, that is being an arsehole. Why are you so determined to believe the worse of me, the worst of this relationship?"

"I heard to you tell her it had always been her. What do you think that did to me, Lucien? It literally ripped my heart out." Alice put her hands over her face. "I can't be here with you again, Lucien. I can't. You broke me last time, it took months to put myself back together and I don't know if I can do that again. If it's Isabelle you want, then you have to go because I am worth more than second best. Why do I always believe the worst? Because it keeps a small part of me safe from ever being broken again."

"Alice there are three things I want more than anything in this life." I said slowly. "To see Hettie again, to know the truth about Ottie and you. You are my life now, Alice. You, not Isabelle…"

"She was the fairy tale, you said it yourself."

"Yes," I said moving towards her and taking hold of her cold hands. "She was the fairy tale, but the story has now changed."

"Has it?"

"Completely."

"In what way?"

"Alice?" I said softly, wrapping my arms around her stiff form. "My happy ending has you in it."

"It does? Why?"

"Because I love you, Alice."

ALICE

"And that's all you said?" Anna asked me from the headstand she was performing on her yoga mat. Toby was noisily eating crisps on the sofa, one eye on Anna's lacy bra, on show due to the tee-shirt that had pooled around her neck, the other eye on a football match. I wondered if he was listening.

"Yeah."

"You said 'oh'? Just like that? As the love of your life told you what you'd been waiting to hear for months, you said 'oh'?"

I nodded and chewed on my lower lip.

"Oh?"

"More like ohhhh, not just 'oh.'"

"Well, that makes it alright then." Anna gracefully lowered her legs and sat crossed legged on the mat. "I mean, it's exactly the right thing to say when someone says they love you. I mean, why would you even want to say it back?"

"Don't." I rubbed my eyes. "Don't say anything else…"

"I mean, shit Alice, that's a deal breaker. This is Lucien. Lucien the control freak who had you tied up in knots for months and the moment he says those three little words, you say 'oh.'"

"In my defence it had been an emotional morning and I was hanging from being in a shitty bar with you. It came out of the blue." I flopped down on the chair. Toby stopped pretending to watch the football. I gave him a *get lost* look but he just grinned and shoved more crisps into his mouth. I pulled a face. "Do you have to listen, Toby, this is girls talk."

"It's interesting."

"How so?"

"Boys don't talk about this shit. We just play football and drink beer…"

"You're such a Neanderthal, how did my best friend end up with a caveman like you?"

"How did my girlfriend end up with a best friend flake like you?"

"Touché!"

"What do you think, Toby? Can you give some 'boy' insight to any of this?" Anna asked, tucking her tee-shirt into her leggings. Toby wiped the side of his mouth and looked disappointed.

"I think she's fucked it right up. Can you get me a beer while you're up?"

"I'm not up."

"Can you get me one anyway?"

Anna rolled her eyes and got to her feet. "He's paying me back for falling in through the door at lunchtime! I should have been at a family dinner, instead I was vomiting in my bedroom bin."

"You're a good friend Anna."

"That I am!" She padded over the polished floor and pushed open the kitchen door. "Do you want a drink?"

"Nope."

"Are you going to see Lucien?"

"Nope."

"Why not?"

"Yeah, why not?" Toby chipped in. His Cheshire cat grin inspired the desire to punch him in the face.

"Because…"

"Because you don't believe him," Anna said suddenly, her eyes boring into mine. "Do you?" She waited for me to speak but I said nothing. "After everything, after him telling you what you've waited months for, you still don't believe him."

I shook my head slowly. "I'm too scared to believe him."

"Why? Because of what you think you heard?"

"I know what I heard, Anna. I'm not a drama queen like…" I stopped speaking but the unsaid word was loud in the air.

"Like who? Me?"

"It has been known." I said, chewing my nail. "He said there was more to it. His conversation with Isabelle, I mean."

"I believe him. Someone in love with his ex would not have tracked you down to that shit hole Xander took us to. Nor would he have driven me home, for me just to slobber all over his expensive car. If he really loved his ex, he wouldn't have done any of that. What happened after he dropped you off? That was hours ago!"

"I got out of his car and ran to the nearest tube…"

"Did he follow you home?"

"Yes." I took a deep breath in and blew it out. Toby sat up straighter in his chair, crisp held inches from his mouth.

"Then you are a bigger dick that I thought." He said. "Men don't do shit like that for someone they just want to fuck."

"She's more than a fuck." Anna said quickly.

"That's what I said."

"No, you didn't, you said…"

Toby crunched a crisp. "I said 'men don't do shit like that for someone they just want to fuck.'"

"Oh." Anna said flopping down on the chair. "Well, Alice, there's your answer."

"I didn't ask a question." I said. "I have to go."

"Where?"

"Do you even need to ask?" Toby said to Anna. "She's now realised that she's a complete dick and is going to fix her massive fuck up."

"Are you?" Anna asked me.

"Your boyfriend is more astute than I've ever given him credit for."

"You're more of a dick than I've ever given you credit for!" Toby grinned good naturedly at me.

"Ah fuck off Toby!" I smiled at him. Picking up my bag I said to Anna, "don't you dare blog about this."

"I won't, I promise."

"Seriously though Alice, what are you going to do if he decides he can't be arsed with your inability to be mature in this relationship?" Toby asked me, opening his can of lager with a hiss.

"What do you mean?"

"I mean, you strop off at every hiccup. He's forty-whatever, he doesn't need that shit, he's not a teenager…"

"Toby!" Anna stormed, "now is not the time."

"Someone has to say it, Anna. She needs to sort it out because I can honestly tell you, us blokes don't like drama, it's a ball ache. You girls are all about the drama, but we don't want it. If you did this to me on a regular basis, we would be over."

"It's always been drama." I said, my voice breaking slightly. "Right from the beginning. Always. I don't know how to do it any differently. Lucien and I have always been explosive, always done things like this, it's not just me who strops, but this time, yes, my fear of losing him and of being with him and, honestly, my fear of him made me react in that way."

"What do you mean, fear of him? Does he hit you? Is he aggressive? Should I be worried?" Anna asked suddenly anxious.

Perhaps she should be worried. Perhaps my fears, suddenly spoken out loud should have made me worried too. Was I in an unbalanced relationship with an unbalanced man? I enjoyed, far too much, the dominant side to him, the invited sexual aggression that he displayed when I was at his mercy. So many times, I'd been bound, naked and kneeling on the floor, waiting for him to do what he chose. Whilst it may have brought mind-blowing, earth-shattering orgasms each time, were we losing the connection during normal, everyday sex?

"Alice?"

"No, he doesn't hit me." I said eventually, "nothing like that. I'm not an abused woman, you don't have to worry. He just dazzles me, confuses me and I worry I have an unhealthy obsession with him. I worry I'm lost in him and, you know, he left me once and I'm terrified it'll happen again. If I believe that he does love me, then I'll open up to that and I'm not sure I'd survive having to get over him again."

"Tell him that then. You can't leave the whole 'I love you' conversation with an 'oh'. Have you considered that he is probably feeling really shit now? You said he never opens up, but now he has and to him it probably feels as though you've thrown it back in his face." Anna said, her tense stance relaxing.

"Mate, I'm telling you, whether you and he are over-dramatic with each other or not, you've literally kicked him in the balls." Toby said matter-of-factly. "Men don't like to share their feelings, it's not cool and he seems to be someone who would rather stick pins in his eyeballs than make himself vulnerable. I'm sorry to say, Alice but you've massively fucked up."

"You're not helping, Toby." Anna said sharply, rolling her eyes and grimacing. "She doesn't need to hear this."

"Yes, she does."

"Fuck, I've got to go." I said feeling my stomach hurtle to my feet.

"Alice are you alright? You look very pale. Do you want a glass of water?"

"No," I shook my head. "No, I just need to sort out this massive mess I've made. Thanks Toby, for an arse you've been very helpful." My dry mouth got stuck on the words as I spoke.

"For a flake, you're welcome."

"Ring me later?" Anna said walking me to the front door of her flat.

"Yeah."

"It'll be fine." She pulled me into a massive hug that nearly forced the air from my lungs. I gripped her tightly, fearing the worst, fearing that I was exactly what Toby had said I was, an immature fuck up.

***

I took a taxi to Lucien's although I couldn't really afford it. After the drunken debacle earlier, I had gone well over the budget I allowed myself. With the move from The Hub impending and the uncertainty of where Saffron and I would end up, I was watching every penny carefully, particularly as I'd blown so much cash on my holiday. But, there was no way I could have faced the long tube journey with the ever growing need to vomit churning my stomach. I'd been a complete fool. Lucien was not a man who gave anything away, he was so measured and controlled and even after following me to St Lucia, he still seemed wary. It's why I held back from him, protected myself from the possibility he could leave me again. I would never forget how I felt in Paris, broken and alone, but my feelings for Lucien ran so deep that sometimes I felt like I was drowning, and it led to moments like this, where I fucked up inordinately.

I handed my card over to the taxi driver and paid the large bill before getting out of the car with such a feeling of dread in my belly I began to see spots in front of my eyes. I took a few deep, steadying breaths, leaning against the front wall of the apartment building, then rang the buzzer. I knew he was in because I could hear music coming from the windows. It took an age for him to answer the door and it was only as I was beginning to walk away, that he opened it.

LUCIEN

"Why are you here?" I asked Alice as she stood looking fearful on the pavement. Her hands were shaking as she held onto her bag and I got a grim sense of satisfaction from her discomfort.

"I came to see you." Her mouth sounded dry and sticky, so much so that I had to strain to hear her speak. Alice's teeth were firmly clamped on her lower lip as she waited for me to say something.

I didn't know what to say. I'd fucking said it all and she slapped me around the face with it, something I genuinely never expected from Alice. I had guessed a long time ago how she felt about me, but I had kept how I felt about her locked under a key of whiskey and dominance. She'd changed me, changed me for the better or so I thought. Alice was the first woman I'd felt anything for since Isabelle and the first time I'd allowed myself to feel something for anyone since Ottie died. Now I wondered if I had gotten it all wrong. Perhaps she should have been able to have a relationship with her fucking blue-eyed hero, then I could have kept myself to my agreements and had none of this shit.

I knew Alice was different. She was a complicated mix of unworldly and streetwise but being with her made me a better person. She'd held my hand during one of the hardest moments of my life, visiting my daughter's grave, trusting me and believing me even when I couldn't do the same. So, I took a leap of faith, told her that I loved her, and it blew up in my fucking face. Right now, I didn't want to be anywhere near her.

"Why?"

"To talk." She said, fixing her gaze on a point on the floor.

"I think everything has been said."

"Not by me."

"I'm not sure I even want to hear what you have to say, Alice."

"Why?" She asked and I watched panic flood her eyes.

"Because you made me feel like a cunt."

"Lucien!" Alice said shocked. "Don't use that word."

"Imagine," I said darkly, "imagine telling someone something so intimate, so intimate in fact, that it took weeks and weeks to acknowledge it even to yourself, something you were sure was

38

reciprocated, only to have the singular response of 'oh'. Imagine what it cost to say those words after a decade of blackness. The blackness that you knew I had inside, eating me up one part of my soul at a time. Your response was to run. Yes, Alice, you made me feel like a cunt."

I felt crazed as anger and humiliation burned through me. I had been right to keep myself away from shit like this, completely right to give into my sexual desires but never give any part of me away. I had thought Alice was the one to heal me, but she left me feeling more broken.

"It wasn't like that." Alice whispered, wiping a tear from her cheek.

"No? What was it like then?" I crossed my arms forming a barrier between us. Alice looked hesitantly at me and licked her lips.

"I am scared." She hung her head as she spoke. "I am scared of you, of how I feel for you, of the idea that you will walk away from me just as easily as you did in Paris. I am scared of what we have, of what it was built on, of who you've been and what I've accepted." Alice lifted her head and stared me straight in the eyes. She looked wary and it bothered me. "I'm scared because how I feel for you is all consuming. It's all I think about. It's obsessive almost, and to hand that much power to someone is frightening and you telling me you loved me was the most frightening thing of all."

"You don't trust me?"

Alice shook her head slowly and said in a voice so low I could barely hear her. "You could take it all away."

"So could you."

"There would be many women waiting to take my place." She said.

"There would be a superhero in green camouflage waiting to take mine."

Alice look startled, as though that had never occurred to her. "I don't think so," she said. "There is no queue at my door." She took a deep breath in, squared her posture and wiped her face. "I didn't realise it would be tit for tat. I came to apologise for my immature and badly handled reaction. I wanted to explain so you understood but I don't think we're going to get anywhere tonight. I think I'll go home. You know where to find me."

Alice turned from me and began to walk along the road. My feet felt leaden and refused to move despite me wanting to stop her. She was right, this had been the worst kind of conversation. "Alice?"

"Goodnight Lucien."

I'd definitely met my match in Alice Addison.

ALICE

"So what are our options?" Saffron asked me, spinning in her chair. The Hub was painfully quiet, many of the cohabites had left for new premises and it felt strange for the large space to be so silent.

"Well, it's back to my flat, I think. We can turn Xander's room into an office, it's less cramped than the kitchen at least. I'll have to move the bed somewhere but…"

"Did Lucien change his mind about the spare office at his?"

"We fell out, I'm not going to assume that offer is still available to us."

"Why?"

"I'm a dick, he's a dick…mostly my fault, some of his fault." I shrugged. I always felt awkward talking about Lucien with Saffron, particularly as she resented him for taking me from Zac. I didn't ever point out that my heart had always belonged to Lucien, because I adored Saffron, she was the best assistant a girl could have, and to lose her would be devastating. We tried to avoid talking about Zac or Lucien, merely acting as though they didn't exist during working hours. It seemed to suit but there was no avoiding the huge elephant in the room and I felt certain it was only a matter of time before we couldn't pretend it wasn't there.

"Hmm." She said and stopped spinning. "Well, one thing is for sure, we don't have a lot of time before we have to move."

"We have a week." The Hub rent was going up astronomically at the end of the month and with limited options I saw us heading back to my flat. There wasn't a lot in Xander's room and the furniture that was there was so minimal that it could be donated to charity without a backwards glance. "I just need to empty the spare room and that would do us for now."

I felt a pull in my chest. I'd started my business in my flat, hiding from the world as I tried to mend my broken heart. I didn't socialise for six long months and whilst I found inspiration from my trips to coffee shops on the high street, I worried that I could easily lose my social self if we moved the business back home again.

It bothered me too that I'd not heard from Lucien since the argument the day before. He had every right to be angry at me, I screwed up massively but there was no respite from the anxiety that had churned my stomach since I walked away from his apartment. I had woken up in a cold sweat as I considered that I may have completely blown it, played the game all wrong and would pay the price with my heart. It had taken a long time to heal after Paris, but this time, having been completely my fault, it would take a lifetime to recover from.

I had checked my phone over and over during the long night and even longer day. I had tried to busy myself, focus on client demands and new quotes I'd had in, but always in the back of my mind was the whispering voice that Lucien and I could very likely be over.

'*Has he phoned yet?*' Anna's text beeped loudly in the quiet. Saffron tried not to look interested as I reached for the phone and read the message.

'*No.*'

'*He will.*' I chucked the phone back on the desk. I could imagine Anna's face when she wrote the message, eyes screwed up and lip chewed. How long should I leave it before waving the white flag.

"Do you want some help? Saffron asked, interrupting my thoughts.

"With what Saff?"

"Emptying the room?"

"Possibly. I'm not sure it's the right move for us, for me. Maybe I need to look for a new Hub?"

"It would be more sociable."

"Yeah." I pushed my chair back and sighed. "I can't concentrate. I'm going on a coffee run because I need some air. Usual?"

"Yes please, but no sugar."

"Really?" Saffron put sugar in everything.

"Yeah, I read an article about sugar being the cause of cancer and dementia and all that shit, I decided to lessen my chances."

"There is sugar in cocktails too you know!"

"I said lessen, not reduce completely!"

I grinned. "One sugarless extra shot cappuccino coming up." I stood up and picked up my bag, a battered rucksack I'd had since university. The straps had frayed with use, but I wasn't quite ready to part with it, not yet. I stuffed my phone into the front pocket and left the section. It saddened me that the Hub was nearly empty. Across the room the copy writers were packing files into big boxes, soon we would be all that were left. It made the move to the spare room all the more likely.

"Arse." I muttered, stomping down the steps, feeling overwhelming frustration at the end of the most fun era I'd had in a while.

"Not the response I was hoping for." Lucien said lightly, from the bottom step. He looked tired and with hair still wet from the shower I assumed he'd not been to the office.

"I was thinking out loud." I said, surprised to see him. "It's too quiet, everyone has left, or is leaving."

"Are you coming to the office then?" He asked casually.

"I don't know."

"Why?"

"I'm not sure how healthy that would be."

"Meaning?"

"It would be too easy to get lost in…never mind. I'm just not sure."

"Get lost in what? The unhealthy relationship you have with me?" Lucien snapped.

"Pardon?" I took a step backwards while my hand involuntarily flew to my chest. My heart was frantic under my palm.

Lucien's face flashed and he looked darkly at me. "Isn't that how you describe it?"

I felt faint, fear at where the conversation was going began to twist my stomach. "Once, maybe."

"More than once, Alice."

I swallowed hard. Lucien glared at me. "Yeah, ok, more than once. It was far from healthy in the beginning Lucien, it wasn't even a relationship, you described it as an agreement. There was nothing remotely healthy about our liaisons, although your other women may have disagreed…"

"Always you bring them up."

"Shit, Lucien what is this?" I demanded, suddenly feeling the panic flip over to anger. "Are you deliberately trying to goad me? To trip me up? To make me fail at some fucked up test? Are you

43

wanting to make me pay for my bad response? Because, honestly, I've been paying for it all night. You want to make me say something that will give you the reason you're searching for to walk away from me? Is that it? Are you looking for a get out clause? I told you before, Lucien. I don't play games. I don't know how to. I know I handled your declaration badly, but I'm scared of my feelings for you. My fear keeps me awake. I could quite easily get so wrapped up in you that my life would pass me by, that is why I am uncertain about taking an office in your building. Because I don't trust me. Me, Lucien. But," I shrugged, "if you want to keep making me pay for my supposed apathy, go ahead, I've not got the time to pander to it. Have a good day."

Lucien sighed and took my arm. "I didn't come here to argue," He said, "I came to tell you that I have a meeting in an hour with Delphine because I didn't want you turning up at the office, seeing her there and thinking..." He stopped.

"Thinking what, Lucien?"

"Oh, I don't know, Alice. Perhaps I didn't want you to think that I was fucking her under my desk."

"She'd probably like that." I sulked visibly and Lucien grinned. In this game we played, he'd won that round.

"Yeah, she probably would."

"Fuck off, Lucien."

"Happy to." He said, his smile widening. "You look really sexy when you're pissed off."

"I'm delighted you think so, particularly as it's only ever you that pisses me off."

"Just think," Lucien said moving closer. "If you moved into the spare office, I could fuck you under my desk all day, every day!"

"Not the most profitable way for me to spend my day." I bristled.

Lucien moved so close that I could almost taste the masculine scent of his skin. "But the most exciting." He lazily rolled his tongue along the underside of my jaw and I felt weakness in my knees. "You smell so good." He murmured, nipping my ear. I closed my eyes and leaned into him.

"You need to go." I whispered.

"Why?"

44

"I have things to do." I moaned softly against his chest.

"I have you to do."

"Later."

"Be at mine, eight o'clock. Don't be late."

Lucien kissed me deeply and was gone before I could even catch my breath. I tried to shut out the whispering voices taunting me with the glamourous images of Delphine, the sex club owner and Lucien's business partner. I hated that he had dealings with her, that his past life was still very much in present and that she personified everything that Lucien used to be. *Maybe it's who he still is.* I watched him walk to his car, parked on double yellow lines at the side of the High Street. I'd no idea if anything had been resolved but being on a promise was good enough.

***

I couldn't think of one reason why I could just turn up at Lucien's office. My mind ticked over and over until Lucien was practically fucking Delphine under his desk and my insecurity began to bubble out of my ears.

'*Fancy lunch?*' I text Bonnie and Clare. I knew I was using them as an excuse to be in Lucien's office, but I hadn't seen them for ages and lunch would be better than sitting at my desk staring into space, picturing Delphine's gorgeous, curvaceous body writhing on top of Lucien's strong, masculine, muscular form. It was driving me crazy.

'*YES!*' Clare replied, her message in big, bold letters. '*Although Bonnie and I are skint, so we'll have to eat here. I'm pretty sure the big boss man won't mind you using our catering facilities!!!!!!!!!*' I grinned at the excessive use of exclamation marks as she punctuated her words.

"Saff, I'm going out for lunch."

"You're really struggling today aren't you?" Saffron commented giving me a long look. "What's he done this time?"

"Who?"

"Lucien! He didn't call, then he turned up, then you went weird, now you're going out. I'm not as dumb as I look, Alice."

45

"I've never said you were dumb." I replied sighing. "It's always complicated with Lucien."

"You're a glutton for punishment, Alice." Saffron said, crunching a carrot stick coated in humous. "You let him get away with everything, it's like you have no pride at all where Lucien is concerned."

I felt my face redden. Saffron shrugged and dipped another piece of carrot into the beige gloop.

"I do have pride." I insisted.

"With work and with yourself, yes you do. With Lucien, not so much."

"Are you still cross about Zac?" I asked her. "Is that what this is all about?"

"No, not at all." Saffron shook her head quickly and her earrings bounced off her cheeks. "I will admit that I'd massively hoped that you and he would hit it off, you're perfect for each other. He's a badass, you're a badass...most of the time anyway, and I was as gutted as Zac that you chose Lucien, but you did and that's fine. But really, Alice, where Lucien is concerned, I'm not always sure you make the right choices."

Saffron looked nervous and I sent a small smile in her direction, mainly to let her know that it was ok she was saying those things. It bothered me that she wasn't the first of the people close to me to comment on Lucien's more domineering personality and that I allowed him to affect everything.

I understood his need for control, it all related to the death of his daughter and the loss of his family, but perhaps I was giving him too much control over me. Maybe it wasn't an equal relationship but one where he walked all over me and I allowed it. Maybe it was time to be stronger, more assertive and less fearful that he would leave me.

He was still here.

He said he loved me. Perhaps now I should just let out the breath I'd been holding for months and put some of me back into our relationship.

Saffron was right. I was a badass. It's about time Lucien saw the real me again.

LUCIEN

Delphine glowered at me. "You cannot be serious, Lucien?"

"I am, Delphine, completely serious." I leaned forward and picked up a brown envelope from my desk. "I had my lawyers draw up the papers. The club is now solely yours."

A flush spread across her cheeks as she reached for the envelope I held out for her. "Why, Cherie?"

"It's time to move on, it was fun, but that kind of fun can't last forever. It's your baby, you earned it."

Delphine pulled the documents from the envelope and crossed her slim legs at the knee as she read the papers. There was no catch, nothing that could be pulled apart by her lawyers, nothing apart from my bold signature giving the rights and future earnings of the club to her. She deserved it. The delinquent sex den where adults could play whatever games they consented to, had been a success due to her hard work and dark desires. She was a sexual deviant, her body designed for any pleasure and having fucked Delphine on more occasions than I could remember, she liked it as sordid as it came. She had been my sexual match. We were a dangerous mix and had we moved beyond a fuck partnership and into a relationship it would have taken us too far into the darkness that neither of us would have survived it.

"It's as much you as it is me." She said looking up from the paperwork.

"Not really."

"Oh come now, Lucien, you couldn't walk away completely."

I'd thrown her. Delphine's English took on a more pronounced French accent when she was upset or angry and from the way she was speaking I had the feeling she was both. I should have forewarned her.

"I have to, Delphine. All good things come to an end." She looked at me through narrowed eyes.

"Is this because of that mousy girl?" The snarl wasn't hard to miss.

"Alice?"

She nodded curtly and her eyes darkened.

"Are you jealous?" I asked lightly. Delphine's flush darkened.

"Of her?" She spat. "Hardly. She's no match for me, she's no match for you either, Cherie. She doesn't think the same, we're different, you and me. She is not like us. She wants to be, but she is not."

"You're talking, of course, of the night she came to you?" I remembered only too clearly, the night I'd safe-worded Alice and run to Delphine. I had no where else to go. The lure of the club, of the ease in which I could forget whilst there, was too much of a pull. Delphine had knowingly taken Alice, promised her the experience of her deepest sexual desires and ensured I had front row viewing as Alice was led to the perverted brethren who would do what they wanted with her. I felt faint, sick and disgusted as I saw her beautiful naked body being lusted over, but she wasn't there long before she fled.

Alice had known I was there.

"Yes."

"I think we both know what you had intended, Delphine." I said, smiling to hide the anger that surfaced with the memory.

She shrugged and ran a long, red fingernail along her plump mouth. "As I said, she is not like us."

"I am not like *us*."

"Ah, Cherie, that is where you are so wrong. You are burying that side of you in this hopeless case of romanticism you are suffering with. You and I, we are not designed for one person because we cannot ever be happy with just one. We enjoy the freedom, the chase, the excitement and eroticism of a nameless fuck with a willing body, the submissive soul who gives in to our perversions."

"Perhaps you are suggesting I need someone like you?" I asked her lightly, watching as she relaxed back into her chair. Delphine knew she was a great fuck. She had dominated me on more than one occasion, having me begging and whimpering on the floor as she unleashed her full power on me. It wasn't something I cared to repeat but served a purpose in the aftermath of the accident.

"You have to admit, Lucien." Delphine said, running her red tipped fingers down her throat to the centre of her generous cleavage. "You and I were unstoppable."

"We were dangerous." I said grinning. "We would have ended up dead."

"Perhaps," she nodded slowly. "but it would have been an incredible way to go." Delphine sighed. "I am sad to be losing you to someone so ordinary."

"There is nothing ordinary about Alice." I said handing her a pen.

"I should have liked to fuck her." Delphine said, taking the pen and flicking through the pages of the document. "She was so promising."

"She is not for sharing." I said as Delphine signed on the line.

"And yet I sense," she replied looking up at me, "you are unsure of her."

"Yes." The admission rang loudly in the air and Delphine smiled knowingly at me.

"Interesting."

"How so?" I asked.

"The power she has. It's as though you are her sub."

"I'm no one's sub, Delphine. You should know that."

"I should, yet of that I am no longer sure." Delphine handed me the paperwork and continued, "I wondered how it makes her feel?"

"How what makes her feel?"

"To know that she has succeeded where all others have failed."

"I'm not sure she even knows."

"This bothers you?"

I ignored the question and Delphine watched me as I crossed the room to file my copy in the cabinet under the drinks bar and put the other copy into a new envelope. I felt unnerved, particularly as her gaze was so heated. I wondered when Delphine would stop wanting me. The pull to the old life was not as strong, but it was there. It was my back up to things falling apart with Alice. She wasn't the only one of us with fears, I had them too. They came to me in the darkness, the screams of my dying daughter punctuating my sleep,

49

but they also now came to me in the light. The hero in khaki taking my girl. I had to have a safety net and I wondered if Delphine was it.

She smiled slowly at me, as I poured two small whiskeys into the crystal glasses on the bar and parted her legs. Delphine wasn't wearing any underwear and the sight of her shaven pussy twitched my cock.

"Are you sure?" She purred, lowering the zip of her top with her glistening fingernail, "are you sure you want to leave it all behind."

For the first time since Alice came back into my life, the temptation was there.

"I'm sure." I was sounding weak. Delphine lowered her zip further and her tanned breast was exposed, the dark nipple hardened in the air-conditioned atmosphere of my office.

"Do you remember," she said, sucking her finger and circling her nipple with the moistened tip. "Do you remember sucking on these? Do you remember how much you enjoyed the taste, of pulling on them like a child suckling its mother? Do you remember fucking them, your cock spilling all over them? Do you remember..." she asked opening her legs wider, her skirt riding up to her hips. "...the feel of my pussy, taking you deep? Look..." Delphine whispered, "look how wet I am for you."

I failed to keep my eyes focused on hers and instead they involuntarily looked down. Her pussy lips were glistening in the light and the wet trail was silver on the tops of her thighs.

"Mr Ross?" Carol's voice was loud through the intercom. "Reception has just told me that Alice has arrived."

Thank God. "Thanks Carol." I said, my finger on the speak button. "Is she coming up?" The semi-erection I had from Delphine's act went down. Delphine's face closed over and she crossed her legs, zipping up her top as she did so. I could feel my relief spread over my face and her look darkened.

"I don't think so, Mr Ross. Reception said she was meeting with the admin girls."

"Can you ask her to come up here, please?"

"Of course." Carol clicked off and I downed the glass of whiskey.

50

"I wonder..." Delphine said softly. "...whether you are as focused on your new life as you protest."

"Never more so." I replied, feeling a coldness wash over me. "I'd never swap what I had with Alice for what went before."

"And yet, your body says otherwise."

"I'm a man, Delphine, there are physical things we can't control, my mind, however, is fully under my control and regardless of your little show, it would never have gone where you thought it would. If you think differently, it just shows how little you know me. I've gone past casual fucks and the temporary high they bring, it's an illusion. I need real life now."

The door opened and I looked up to see Alice walk in.

"Hi." She said looking between Delphine and me.

"Hi." I said softly. Delphine glared at me before standing up to greet Alice. I watched as Alice took in Delphine's barely-there suit, the low top designed to taunt, the short skirt that skimmed the tops of her tanned legs. Alice's face fell as she tucked her tee-shirt into the worn jeans. To me, Alice looked far more appealing than Delphine in her overly-sexy outfit, but she would not feel the same.

"Alice!" Delphine said brightly. "Delightful to see you."

"Hello Delphine." She replied flatly.

"What a surprise to see you." Delphine was taunting Alice, knowing, as I did, that Alice was bound to have turned up here, feeling uncertain and worried. I hated that she felt that way but more so, I hated that Delphine had me questioning both myself and my loyalty. I would do whatever it took to not lose Alice, but the old version of myself was risking it at every turn.

"I'm lunching with friends." Alice said quietly. "I hadn't planned to come up here."

"Perhaps there was a reason that you weren't aware of?" Delphine asked huskily. "Perhaps a curiosity? Or desire?" She turned to me and I was suddenly nervous by the look in her eyes. "We were just talking about desire, weren't we, Lucien?"

"Something like that!" I shifted, uncomfortable with where the conversation was headed. It was a slight movement, but Alice noticed, and her eyes widened. "I was signing over the Paris club to Delphine." Alice didn't believe me.

51

"Oh?" She said, not taking her eyes from mine. "Is that all?"

"What did you think, Cherie? That Lucien and I were fucking like old times?" Delphine asked.

Alice shrugged and smiled. Her hands were shaking but her resolve was fierce. "Anything is possible, Delphine, but these days, Lucien doesn't like things so…" She looked Delphine up and down. "…obvious."

With a deliberate slowness Delphine turned and bent over, lower than was needed, to pick up the envelope she'd discarded on the chair. Alice's mouth fell open, horrified, when she saw the nakedness beneath Delphine's skirt.

"What the fuck?" She whispered, looking at me. "What the fuck are you playing at, Delphine?"

"It's not what you think?" I said, moving towards her. Alice put her hands up as though keeping me back.

"You sure about that, Lucien?" She sneered. "Don't you think it's funny that it is never, ever what I think, is it?"

Delphine stood watching us, a slow smile curving her lips. "Alice, Alice, Alice, so mistrusting."

"Fuck off, Delphine." Alice snapped, "this is between Lucien and me."

"Feisty!" Delphine purred. "I wonder, are you as feisty in the bedroom?"

The slap came from nowhere. Alice's palm hit Delphine's cheek before either of us had seen her move. The sound rebounded around the room as Delphine's hand cupped her cheek, pain flitting across her face followed by anger so intense I had no idea what her next move would be. I'd always been able to read Delphine, she and I were almost cut from the same cloth, but in that moment, I drew a blank. I didn't know what to expect. Alice looked shocked. Her eyes darted to me and I blew out a loud breath.

"Don't make an enemy of me, Alice." Delphine said crossing the room to me. "It's not wise." She kissed me, her tongue darting into my mouth. It felt strange to have another mouth on mine, even though it lasted seconds. I pulled away and saw the distress on Alice's face.

"Alice!"

"What the fuck…" She choked. "You absolute bitch!" Alice glared at Delphine. "What do you think this will achieve? You want Lucien, is that it? Or you want to beat me? What is it? Did Lucien reject the life that had you in it?" She flicked the envelope that Delphine held in her hand. "Or are you pissed that I walked out of your charade in Paris? Women like you Delphine, are a cancer on the rest of us. I can only imagine what you hoped for today, but you won't get it. You can torment me as much as you want, because I will always be better than you."

"How so?" Delphine growled, her head to one side. "What makes you think that? I had Lucien so turned on his cock was hard just moments before you arrived…"

How Alice kept her pain from showing, I'd never know but she did. She stood firm and said, "it doesn't take much to make a man hard, Delphine, but they are not always tempted although I wonder how many men would keep it in their pants to keep you."

Alice looked at me before turning on her heel. "I can't be doing with this shit. I've got a lunch date. You two can sort yourselves."

With a slam of my glass office door, Alice was gone.

"I suggest you leave now, Delphine, and don't come back." I said icily. "You may make a bad enemy but to make an enemy of me would be the worst mistake you could ever comprehend. Take the club, take the papers and leave. Now."

"Cherie," Delphine said silkily, "you will be back. You always come back, it's who you are!"

"No," I corrected her. "It is who I was. Alice is who I am now."

"Then you are a fool."

ALICE

My hands shook all through lunch. Clare and Bonnie didn't seem to notice that anything was wrong as they chattered away. Former colleagues came to say 'hi' and ask me about my business. It felt good to be back inside the warmth of Lucien's workforce, yet Delphine played heavily on my mind, almost as heavily as Isabelle. She didn't hold the power though, Lucien had never loved her, but she made me nervous. She was the first woman on his path of self-destruction following the accident that killed Ottie and the first one to show him the role of a Dom. That is the only reason she bothered me, because she would be waiting if we failed.

There would be no one waiting for me. Lucien may have thought Zac would be there to take his place, but I'd not seen him since the Awards dinner and had stopped listening for the roar of his motorbike. I was unsure what I would say to him if I saw him now but sometimes I wondered how much more secure I would have felt being with him than I did with Lucien.

I walked back to the Hub feeling emotionally beaten. My palm still smarted from hitting Delphine, although I did have a sense of satisfaction from having slapped her. It was very unlike me. I usually ran away from any kind of trouble and hitting someone wasn't how I normally resolved my issues. I justified it to myself because Delphine was a conniving bitch who had either expected to have fucked Lucien under his desk, or to rile me. All things considered, being riled was my preferred option but I couldn't stop thinking about what could have been. He had been turned on, of that I was sure. Any man being faced by a voluptuous and willing female with a bare pussy would have found it hard to have closed their mind to the blatant sexual display. It didn't hurt in the same way as hearing Lucien admit his feelings to Isabelle, but it made me feel sick. Delphine was everything I wasn't, and no amount of sexual preening could change that.

"Good lunch?" Saffron asked as I stomped into our section. The copy writers had cleared their area while I was out, and we were all that remained. I felt sad.

"It was ok." I said, sitting down. "I can't believe we're all that's left in here, Saff."

"I know. You need to make a decision, Alice because we're almost homeless." Saffron leaned back in her chair. "Three quotes came in while you were out and Jefferson Moss paid, so the account is up to date."

"Good news!" I grinned. "We can eat! I don't know what we should do Saffron, there are pros and cons to every option."

"It's free at Lucien's." Saffron said, crossing out some tasks on her list. "That would be a bonus, and he has a gym and a canteen and a receptionist, we could be rich, thin and fed!"

I nodded. "There is that, but, ah I don't know Saff, I wonder if it's just too close to my personal life. Nothing comes for free..."

"Honestly, Alice. Being in your flat, as lovely as it is, is even closer to your personal life. We would only have each other and as much I as I love you, that would be stifling. You and I need people, look how bad it was for your mental health the last time."

"There was more to it than that!"

"I know!" Saffron exclaimed, "I know there was shit going on with Lucien and you were heartbroken and blah, blah, blah, but even so, it's not the right move for us. I've been checking the ads for office space and hot desk space and the prices are extortionate. It would wipe out the profit we make in a second. Lucien's office is our best option, Alice..."

"Nothing comes for free though, Saffron."

"Then pay him the same rent as you pay here. I can't imagine he'll take it, he's loaded, he won't need your few hundred quid, but it will make you feel better and, quite honestly, if the men who work for him are as hot as you say they are, I'll get laid and feel better too! Win, win!"

I laughed. "That's quite the sales pitch. What happened to whatshisname that you had a thing for?"

"He turned out to be a dick, it's the story of my life." Saffron groaned. "I'm destined to walk this life alone!"

"You're twenty-three."

"And?"

"And, there is plenty of time."

"Tell that to my ovaries."

"Saffron?"

"Yeah?"

"Do you need a cocktail?"

"Hell yeah!"

***

I felt nervous walking up the stairs to Lucien's apartment. It had been a complete rollercoaster the past couple of days and I couldn't be sure of the reception I was going to get. Part of me expected Delphine to be on the sofa, draped in black leather, waiting for Lucien to end things with me so she could stake her claim.

I let out a sigh of relief that Lucien was waiting for me, the door wide open, when I climbed the last set of stairs. There was soft lighting behind him, omitting a pale-yellow glow and I could hear the music, quiet enough to just be background noise, drifting from the lounge to the hallway outside.

"Hi." I said, suddenly feeling shy.

"Hey you!" He smiled the slow, sexy smile that I loved. "You're late."

"Sorry, I was waylaid by a cocktail or two with Saffron."

"You drink too much!"

"Yes, at times I'd agree with you." Lucien stood aside to let me into the apartment and followed me in, closing the door behind me. He'd lit candles and the aroma of food filled the air. "You've made dinner?"

"It's been known!" Lucien laughed, a light, musical laugh. "I thought after all the dramas that have hit us recently, I could wow you with my culinary skills and you'd melt like putty in my hands!"

"Oh, I see," I smiled up at him. "You think the way to my heart is through my stomach, rather like a man!"

"Something like that!" Lucien paused and a visible spark zipped between us. He raised my hand to his lips and dropped a kiss on my knuckles. "I just wanted to show you how much you mean to me. Everything has conspired against us these past few days and it's all because of me, because of who I am and who I've been. I know you

56

deserve more than that, more than me. You didn't deserve to hear my conversation with Isabelle and you certainly didn't deserve all that shit with Delphine. You're better than the life I used to lead, and it wouldn't surprise me if one day you realised it and walked away."

"I'm not going anywhere…"

"Not yet, perhaps."

I linked my fingers with his. "I'm really not going anywhere."

"Alice…"

"Shhh," I said, "don't say anything, just kiss me."

Lucien leaned forward and wrapped his spare hand in my hair, pulling my head back until I was looking up at him. "I was completely lost until you came into my life," he whispered. "You're my guardian angel."

"What about Isabelle?"

"Isabelle? She's my past…"

"Do you still love her?"

There was a long pause and I could hear my blood pounding in my ears as I waited for him to speak. "I love you, Alice Addison." Lucien dropped light kisses on my mouth, and I wrapped my arms around his shoulders, feeling the muscles of his torso digging into my skin. "It's only you."

"And Delphine?"

"Delphine is a tease, a lost soul like I was before you came along. Everything she did today was to prove herself, to prove she was desirable and powerful only it did the opposite."

"She's so sexy," I whispered back, dragging my eyes from his and swallowing hard. "She's everything I'm not. She was half naked in your office, Lucien. She tempted you."

"I was never tempted by her. I'm not going to lie to you, my body responded to her little show, but not my mind, that was never in question. Delphine wanted a reaction, she wanted to believe she held the control, that's all she did it for. Alice, Delphine was an escape once upon a time, but these days she's everything you don't need to be."

"Really?"

"Alice, the only person you need to be is you. The only person I want to see when I open my eyes, is you." Lucien sighed. "I didn't think I would ever come back from the depths of hell and then there was you. Lovely, sassy, gobby you who could chase the shadows away. You have to stop worrying and stop believing the worst of me, just have some faith, Alice. I'm not going anywhere. I can't."

"Why?"

"Because my life would be nothing without you in it." Lucien kissed my lips softly.

His words, filled with so much honesty and meaning, overwhelmed me and I felt a prickling of tears behind me eyes. I'd waited so long to hear him say those words, that they were hard to take in but as Lucien stared down at me with a fire raging in his brown eyes, there was no disputing that he meant them. I could see the truth in his face, in the silver of the scar that marred his cheek and the curve of his full mouth.

I felt the same heat that he did. It held us together, like the ends of magnets searching for its opposite. We were opposites, but that's what made us right. We were right.

I leaned up on my tiptoes and kissed Lucien's full mouth. "Tell me again," I whispered against his lips.

"I love you Alice." Lucien ran his tongue lightly over my lips and sparks bounced over my skin.

"I love you too."

***

LUCIEN

The ice cream tasted all the more sweet when licked from Alice's hot, aroused nub. Her wet, silken sex gripped my fingers as I slid them into her, first one, then two, then three until she was filled, my tongue never leaving the bud, hidden beneath its hood. She writhed under me, moaning softly as I licked and sucked her, fucking her channel with my fingers. When I teased the delicate skin of her arse with my thumb, Alice let out an involuntary gasp and a red flush coloured her cheeks. She was ashamed of her dark desires. Alice still struggled with the pleasure her body got from our play, and while I tried not to push her, knowing how much I turned her on always got me hard.

Achingly so.

It felt different this time.

More intense. The feel of Alice's body under me, the wetness that flowed from her, the sounds of pleasure that escaped her lips were all so different. It was the confession of feelings, the confessions of the truths that had weighed us down, the promises that came with those truths.

I meant every word.

My life would be nothing without her in it. The path I had been on was dangerous, all-consuming and dark. My twisted actions and the twisted women I played with would have eventually broken what remained of my humanity and I would have been lost, drunk, alone and stuck in a never-ending cycle of absolute self-loathing. Meeting Alice brought me back. Too many times I'd come close to losing her, but somehow I'd held onto her. She believed in me, trusted me, even when I couldn't do the same for myself. Alice looked at me with a knowing eye and kept me moving forward.

Now her beautiful body was committed to mine and her beautiful soul was intertwined with mine, through the three words we'd uttered, the three words that brought the sunshine even on the darkest days – *I love you.*

I'd not said it for a decade, since Isabelle left and probably long before that. We had got so lost in ourselves that the marriage was over way before the accident. The recriminations followed me for years. So much anger and so much heartache that I had blamed myself for, but since Alice, I had begun to question how much of it was fault.

I was alive because of Alice.

I would find Hettie, because of Alice.

Her body was glistening in the soft lighting, moist from the effort of holding her orgasm in. She tasted so delicious as I slowly licked her, nipping and sucking at the swollen nub until her cries filled the room.

"Lucien, please." She begged, "please I'm going to cum."

I took my fingers from inside her. "Not until I say so."

I loved the games she enjoyed to play, the control she exerted to keep me happy and the control I exerted to bring her the most intense orgasms she could bear to give in to. A couple of times she had fainted with the power of her orgasm, so I was careful not to take her too far. It thrilled me that my touch could have her trembling, that my words could make her melt and the pull between us got stronger each time.

I stopped looking when I met Alice.

"Turn over." I said gruffly. Alice couldn't stop the disappointment that she wasn't going to cum on my tongue, from spreading over her face. I didn't comment, merely gripped her hands behind her back and wrapped them in cuffs. She winced as her shoulders were held tighter than was comfortable but said nothing. "The safe word, Alice, remember the safe word."

She'd never used it but every time we played, I reminded her. I suspected she would never use it, as I had done so in Paris. She wasn't afraid of me, not like I was of her. I was afraid of her power, of how much she was under my skin and the only time I'd used the safe word, I had broken us both. *Red, Alice. Red.*

I raised her hips and pushed cushions beneath her groin. Her arse was lifted, her pussy bare and I took time to admire the view, the silken trails of her juice wet on her thighs. She was so fucking sexy, so fucking willing that my cock twitched and ached as it hardened until it was unbearable. Never once taking my eyes from her, I pleasured myself until my cock erupted with hot cum all over her arse. "You look fucking dirty with my cum dripping from you." I breathed in her ear as I lowered the eye mask onto her face.

Alice bit down on her lower lip and said nothing. I smiled to myself. She was good. No, scrap that, she was fucking amazing. She fulfilled my every desire and made me cum harder than I ever had before. It had truly been a great day when Alice Addison walked into my office.

I wiped my cock down and then cleaned up the mess I'd made on her arse before taking a breath in. My orgasm had fogged my mind and I needed a moment to focus. I took a few more steadying breaths and looked down at Alice. "What to do with you." I said huskily. "What shall I do?"

The new toys were laid out on the sofa. Alice had seen them, approved them, had been excited by them. Brand new and just for her. Only ever to be used on her. She'd liked that. Alice had shivered as I laid them out, allowing her to choose the ones she wanted to use. Some were beyond her experience and I'd put them back into the crate and away in the cupboard. They were for another day. Maybe.

I warmed the small bottle of oil between my palms as Alice lay silently waiting for me. Unscrewing the top, I dribbled the oil onto her lower back, watching as it ran along the hollow and down between her arse cheeks before pooling onto the floor. It was warm enough to feel pleasant, so I drizzled more, rubbing it into her arse cheeks as she pushed against my hands. "Stop, Alice. Don't move or I will spank you." I felt her smile in the air as she pushed once more. Then I gave her what she wanted. The spanks rang out, but Alice said nothing. Not a sound came from her, but she had visibly relaxed.

She was fucking amazing.

I rubbed my palm to reduce the sting and smooth my hands back over her cheeks. She didn't move this time but tensed as I spread her legs wider and pressed my finger against the forbidden hole. "Shall I?" I murmured. "Shall I fuck it?"

"No." Her reply was barely audible.

"No?"

"No, Sir."

61

I reached behind me and selected the first toy, a small silver plug, its jewelled end sparkling in the low lighting. I lubricated it between my oiled hands and slowly pushed it into Alice's arse.

"Ah." She sighed as it went in as far as was safe. I watched her redden, her lower lip immediately clamped between her teeth as she tensed around the toy.

"Relax, Alice." I whispered. "This is for you, your pleasure, your most delinquent of desires…" Then I flicked the tiny switch and the plug began to softly vibrate against the delicate walls of her taboo channel.

Alice pulled at the cuffs holding her hands behind her back, but they held firm and all she could do was moan as desire dominated her shame.

ALICE

I shouldn't like it but the pulsing deep within me was so arousing and so dirty that I felt my pussy convulse. It took more strength than I knew I possessed to hold back my orgasm and I tried to shut my mind to the sexy device that was sending waves of pleasure through me. I liked it. Lucien was right. I was a dirty girl.

I knew what toys to expect, I'd chosen them, so nothing would be a shock, but when Lucien pushed a dildo into me and set it vibrating, at odds to the one in my arse I thought I would explode. It was too much and not enough. Deeply erotic and desperately mortifying. My head spun faster than my mind could keep up and I saw spots of blackness behind my eyes.

"Lucien…" There must have been something in the way I spoke that had him pulling the dildo from me.

"Too much?"

I nodded.

"Use the safe word, Alice."

"No. I don't want to."

"Slower?" He asked me.

"Yes please, sir."

Slowly, and with a smaller pulse, Lucien slid the dildo back into me and my tight muscles held it in place.

"You look beautiful." He murmured, stroking his fingers along my spine. "So beautiful like that."

I pulled against my restraints as his hands cupped my arse. The beat within me banged like a bass drum – boom, boom, boom – forcing the lava around my body as everything heightened, my senses, my feelings, the longing for more and the guilt for wanting it.

"Shall I fuck you, or make you wait? Hmm, choices, choices," he taunted. "Or shall I play some more. Can you take more, sweet Alice? Can you wait? Shall I see how long I can leave you desperate for the release, Alice?"

I groaned as the pulsing intensified. I needed something to ground me, to keep me from exploding as the fire raged inside me but Lucien had taken his hands from me and I felt raw, exposed and insatiable. There could be no one else for me. No one could ever make me feel this way, to feed the fire with the sexual oxygen that it needed to thrive.

When the suede ends of the flogger hit my skin, my channels clenched around the devices that pulsated and teased. It stung but I craved more, so like the first time in the Cotswolds, yet so different. This was my flogger, chosen for me, bought for me by the man I loved, who loved me and whose own desire was outweighed by his need to bring pleasure to me. I couldn't hold my cries back as the ends bit my flesh. It felt good. It was the grounding I needed as I held back on my orgasm, holding it tight inside despite the burning lava that raced around my veins. I wasn't going to be able to hold it for long and the black spots behind the eyes covered by the mask were dancing uncontrollably.

I had no intention of using the safe word but as Lucien teased and tormented me with the flogger, it was edging nearer and neared to my lips. It would disappoint him if I said it, and for me, it would bring Paris back into our lives and that was a time I longed to forget. Instead I yanked the cuffs and said his name. My voice was weak, my energy was slowly leaving me as my body struggled to cope with the intensity of the play. "Lucien…Lucien." I whispered.

He heard me. He listened to me. He realised I would never safe word him, I wasn't scared, but I was drained, and I couldn't hold on.

"I have to cum." I mumbled, "I have to. I can't hold it. Please, please let me cum." Tears wet the mask as my body trembled once and gave way to an orgasm that ripped through me. I could feel my channel soak the dildo and spill out onto my legs. I feared Lucien would be angry, or upset, that I couldn't wait for him to finish his play, but the black spots were dancing too fast and I could barely breathe.

"Alice!" Lucien said suddenly panicked and pulled the two devices from my body. I slumped against the cushions as he ripped the mask from my face and released the cuffs. Lucien rubbed my shoulder and kissed my back, small kisses along my spine and down to the hollow. "I'm sorry." He whispered. "I'm so sorry, it was too much…"

"No, no it wasn't, it was fine. It was more than fine, it's just…"

"Too much? Why didn't you safe word me? You know the rules, Alice, it's to keep you safe."

"I wasn't in danger." I smiled weakly. "It wasn't unsafe, it was just too intense, and I thought I would pass out if I didn't let go. I'm so sorry, Lucien." I hung my head. "I'm sorry I wasn't strong enough."

Lucien wrapped himself around my naked body and held me tightly too him. "You are stronger than you know, Alice. In so many ways. You are exceptional. Everything about you is exceptional."

"Everything?" I murmured rubbing my back against him.

His cock hardened slowly against my spine and I turned over, wrapping my leg around his hip so his cock lay against my sex.

"Surely you're not ready to go again?" Lucien asked me with wide eyes.

"You'd better believe it!" I said as my tired body woke up. I guided him into me and sighed as he filled me. "You turn me on so much, Lucien, I could go all night."

***

I woke up entangled in Lucien's sheets, my body aching and exhausted from the intensity of the play that was the prologue to a night filled with sex. I was insatiable where Lucien was concerned, but so was he. He taunted and teased me, made love to me, and fucked me so hard I though my head would explode. As we slowly fell asleep together, his arms encircling me tightly, I didn't believe we had anything left to overcome, or anything left to prove to one another.

Lucien was as excited by me as I was by him. It ran deeper than our physical need for one another, it was our souls and our minds. We were linked. He loved me and I loved him, it was all-consuming, powerful, strong and, for me, it was forever. There could be no man who could make me feel this deeply again, even if Lucien and I didn't make it to the end.

It was only him.

I stretched and reached out for his warm body, but the bed was empty. I sat up and gingerly moved my tired body until I was standing. I had faint bruises on my wrists from the cuffs and when I turned in front of the mirror, there was evidence of the flogger on my back. I grinned. Fuck, I loved being dirty. Loved being at his mercy and feeling my body respond. He turned me on immeasurably and just looking at my skin, and the marks our play had left, swelled my body. I was ready for him.

I opened the bedroom door and without covering my aroused nakedness, I walked along the corridor to the lounge. I could hear Lucien talking and, turning the door handle, I opened it cautiously. He was standing in front of the window that looked out over the park, his back to me. He was naked from the waist up, the muscles in his back knotted and tense.

"Are you sure?" He asked the person on the end of the phone, his voice urgent and wavering. "You're absolutely sure?"

Lucien listened to the tinny voice on the end of his phone.

"Can you get the me the address?" He asked, typing onto the tablet on the windowsill in front of him. Lucien waited and then said, "thanks John. I owe you." He paused for the response and then replied, "yes I think it would be good if you went first, just to see. I don't know how the land will lie and I don't want to blow it. Thanks mate, thanks more than I can say." Lucien ended the call and blew out a loud breath.

"Lucien?" I asked tentatively, pulling a throw from the chair nearest me to cover myself. It didn't feel like the moment to be naked. There was a tension in the air that I knew wasn't related to me, but to the phone call I'd partly overheard. My heart thudded in my chest as I waited for him to finish tapping on the tablet. Then he turned to face me.

"That was John, my PI. He's been working for me since Isabelle vanished with Hettie."

"And?" I asked, pulling the throw tighter around me. I knew Lucien didn't have romantic feelings for Isabelle anymore, but she still made me nervous and the mere mention of her name twisted my stomach. Lucien's mission to find her and be reunited with his daughter, was his absolute motivation and when he did, Isabelle would have a permanent place back in his life. I wanted, more than anything, that Lucien could know the truth about the death of Ottie, and his role in the accident that claimed her life. I desperately wanted him to be back with Henrietta, knowing how much of a gap in his life she had left. Some nights Lucien woke me screaming, the anguished cries for his children, pierced the darkness. I held him, comforted him, used my body to calm him, but I knew that until he found Hettie and until he could lay the ghosts to rest, the demons would keep coming until they broke him completely.

LUCIEN

Alice stood silently waiting for me to speak but I didn't know how to put my feelings into words. The clock ticked as the silence between us got louder and louder.

"Lucien?" She pressed moving towards me, looking uncertain. "What did he say?"

I raked my hands through my hair and coughed to clear my throat. The emotions and the flood of hope that came with my feelings, blocked my airway until it burned to breathe. There was hope and yet still I had such a long way to go. John had to take the first step because I wasn't brave enough.

"He has a lead on Jean-Claude. There is a hospital in Switzerland where he worked or may still work…the information is unclear at the moment. It may be a coincidence, but if it is him, then he has changed his last name, I don't know why, maybe to hide from me…whatever the reason, if it's him then we are one step closer."

"That's amazing."

"It's terrifying." I whispered, suddenly afraid. "I've hidden behind the search for all these years, hidden behind bad choices, whiskey and a workaholism that kept me alive, but if it's him, if they're there…" My words tailed off. Alice stared at me, her arm reaching out despite the distance we were standing apart in the lounge. She wanted to help, to be by my side, but I felt enclosed in a bubble that was slowly suffocating me.

"It's a start," she said putting her arm down and crossing the lounge. "It's a puzzle piece, the one you've been looking for. It might fit, Lucien, or it might help you find the next piece, whatever it is, you have to be brave. It's one step closer to the answers."

"I can't go."

"I understand that. I assume John is going?"

"Yes."

"Do you want me to go with him?" It must have taken a lot for Alice to ask as she looked uncertain as the words left her mouth. Could I ask such an enormous undertaking of her? She smiled at me and wrapped her arms around my neck, holding me to her warmth.

"I can't ask you to do that." I said softly, breathing in the floral scent of her skin.

"You didn't."

I hid my face in her neck and gripped her tightly. The delicate perfume of her body grounded me and calmed the rising anxiety in my stomach. I was a lucky man to have met her, someone who was always quick to defend me from myself and the fog from my past.

"What did I do to deserve you?" I said, breathing in the soft scent of her skin. "You are too good for me."

"Lucien? The trip..." She dropped a tiny kiss on my neck. "I can go with John..."

"No!" I said, sharper than I intended but the idea of Alice leaving me with my demons was not an option. Not yet anyway. She looked up at me, startled. "It may yet be a dead end and it may not even be them..."

"Do you believe that?" She asked, letting me go and readjusting the throw she had wrapped around herself.

"I'm scared to hope. It's been so long, Alice, would I even recognise Hettie? Would she recognise me? I don't know her, she's has a life in which I've played no part, would she even want to know me?"

"You're her dad, of course she'd want to know you."

"I killed her sister..."

"You don't know that, Lucien, not for sure." Alice paused and looked thoughtful. She held her hand up to stop me speaking. "I know what you think you did, but I am not convinced."

"Why?"

"Because you don't lose control."

"I do, Alice and you know I do. You've picked me up each time I've lost it. I drove drunk to your flat. Look at how I behaved in Paris." She coloured slightly and I wished I'd not said anything. I shook my head. "I don't want to go over old ground with you, but I was perfectly capable of doing what Isabelle accused me of..."

"You said you hadn't drunk anything that evening. Why don't you believe yourself?"

Alice looked at me with such trust in her eyes. She was so quick to believe that I could never feel for her what I said I did, but her faith in my innate goodness was unwavering. It filled me with dread that I would destroy that faith. What would happen to us when she found out what I knew – that there was a darkness in me that led me to take the life of my daughter. I had always vowed I'd never be like my father, a drunken waste of space who spread rot over everything he touched – but I was more like him than the good man Alice believed me to be.

"Stop dwelling, Lucien!" Alice chided me, crossing the room to the door at the back of the lounge. "You'll have answers soon. I think you'll just need to be more patient than you have ever been before." Alice dropped the throw onto the chair and wiggled her arse. "Now, I'm off for a bath and I'm pretty sure there is room for two."

She always knew how to cheer me up.

***

Saffron glared at me from under her bright yellow fringe. "Alice is busy, Lucien. She is at a client meeting which I've told you every five minutes so far this morning."

"Well, how long will she be?"

I'm pretty sure she muttered *for fuck's sake* under her breath and on any other day, I wouldn't have blamed her. I didn't sleep well last night, despite spending the entire afternoon the day before, exploring Alice's sensational body. Normally that much sex would have sent me into a coma, but she went home, and the darkness enveloped me without her there to push it away. I went for a run at two am but even the fast pounding of the pavements couldn't bring the sleep I desperately needed. I waited for the sun to rise and, after a shower hot enough to warm my over-tired body, I went to the office.

I had too much work to do. I was bidding for a US Navy contract and the entire team were working overtime to get the bid prepared, but since my phone call with John, I could think of nothing but Hettie.

I needed Alice. I needed her near me so that I could breathe. My throat was permanently constricted, and it didn't matter how much water I drank, my mouth was parched. Over and over I could hear

John's voice, *I think we've found them.* It was too risky to hope but without hope I had nothing, apart from Alice.

I watched how she lived her life. She seemed to dance through the days, surrounded by people who valued her. I knew she was still fearful of me and that I had a power over her that didn't always sit comfortably with me. Of course, there were times where that power pleasured us both, but she was wary and she had every right to be, whatever she said to the contrary, it didn't change anything. Underneath there was a darkness and one day it would pull me under. I just didn't want to take Alice with me.

ALICE

My meeting went on and on and on and on… It was worth a lot of money to me, so I drank endless coffees, ate endless biscuits and tried to look interested as the CEO of the tech company droned on. The room was desperately hot and sweat was beginning to pool in my bra. I shifted in my seat and willed him to finish up. I wondered how Lucien was doing. I left his apartment early evening the day before for dinner with Xander. I wanted to stay, the conversation with John Frank had really shaken Lucien up, but he was insistent that he would be fine. I had deliberated going back to his after the meal, but when he didn't answer my calls, I went home.

I didn't have the worry that he would do something foolish. It was more a concern for him, and a wish that he would keep hoping and not give up, even if it would have been easier too. I knew how much finding Hettie meant to him and I also knew, even if Lucien didn't, that he would struggle to move his life onwards until he had confirmation of where she was. I had meant it when I offered to go with John to Switzerland, but I did it for good reason. I wanted to see how the land lay before Lucien had to confront his past and possibly his daughter.

Sometimes I watched him when he didn't see me looking and searched him for the man he said he was. Lucien was a lot of things, some not so positive, but despite his faults, I could not see beyond my belief that he would not have put his children in harm's way. There was more to it, of that, I was certain.

"So, Miss Addison…"

"Alice, please." I had jumped when the CEO's voice cut through my thoughts. I'd told him a number of times to use my first name, but he had a strange chivalry that didn't seem to fit with modern London. It was nice at first but was beginning to grate.

"Miss Addison, we were very impressed with your pitch, and you, winning the London City Award for Outstanding Young Entrepreneur, is no mean feat, particularly in a business as new as yours. However, for such a small business, you are too expensive, which makes you uncompetitive. We have had pitches from vastly more experienced designers who are charging less money. Can you re do your figures which will enable you to compete with them?"

For four hours I'd been sat in that room, selling my soul to a short-sighted money man. "Mr Richards," I said smiling a smile I didn't mean. "I am more expensive because it is a reflection of the work I do. I don't cut corners and I don't rush my projects because I value my clients. That is why I won the award and that is why I get recommended." I shrugged. "If you want someone because they are cheap, I'm not your girl." I stood up with my hand extended. "Thank you for inviting me here and for taking the time to hear my pitch. I don't think my company can give you what you need at the price you want to pay but I do hope you are successful in securing a new designer."

"Now don't be hasty Miss Addison."

"Mr Richards, I would like to win your business and if I did, you would be assured of my commitment to the project. However, I'm not going to lower my price for you. I'll show myself out."

I'd never left a meeting before, but it felt empowering. He had been trying to assert a dominance over me, but the only man who'd ever been able to do that was Lucien. Certainly not the piggy eyed, chubby CEO who had been sitting beside me. I'm not sure how awake the Marketing Manager was, nor the Finance Director who had both joined us a couple of hours ago, but they sat up as I crossed the room.

"Miss Addison," Mr Richards said rubbing his hand across his perspiring brow. "You certainly put up a good argument."

I stopped with my hand on the door handle and grinned. "I also do a great design, Mr Richards. You'll find out when you give me your business."

"I like you, Miss Addison. You have spunk."

"I'll take that as a complement, good day."

It was a strange feeling to let the door close behind me, leaving the three men sitting there looking at each other. I'd presented well and it had been a great pitch, Saffron and I had worked hard on it and we certainly couldn't have added anything else. If they wanted cheap, well fine, but cheap wasn't us. I had never tried to undercut any other design company to win business, mainly because my talent was the one thing I had complete faith in, and because of that faith the business accounts were healthy. Saffron and I gave each client's brief everything we could, some nights we worked well into the small hours and crawled back into the office at first light to make sure every target and every deadline was met. Of course, we would finish early, treat ourselves to expensive cocktails or take random days off once a project was finished and before we had to the start the next one. The Young Entrepreneur Award kept business knocking on our door, but it wouldn't last forever and by then we would be reliant on reputation.

I wasn't sure what kind of reputation I would get having walked out of a big meeting. I felt tired and hungry for something more substantial than the over-rich biscuits I'd been fed all morning. The effects of the conference room coffee were also wearing off, so I crossed the road, skirted round the underground station and walked into the nearest restaurant.

It was a complete surprise to see Zac sitting alone at a table.

"Hi!" I said, startled, feeling my cheeks colour a little.

"Hello, Alice." Zac said standing up quickly and knocking his glass over. The water spilled across the table and began to drip in a steady stream onto the floor. A waiter, passing, stopped to mop up the mess as Zac continued to look awkward. "How are you?" He asked, reaching his arm up to scratch his jaw.

"Good. Yeah, good thanks, fine." I'd forgotten how handsome he was, a light, open face and kind eyes with crinkles around them. I felt strange as I suddenly remembered how it felt to have his lips on mine, it had been nice, gentle and had there not been the raw primal pull to Lucien, Zac would have been enough for a lifetime. For a lucky woman, he would be the perfect match, and had I not ever met Lucien, for me he would have been just right. "How's life on the edge?"

"Edge like!" Zac grinned and said gently, "this feels more awkward than I'd expected."

"Yeah." I pulled a face. "It shouldn't feel awkward, should it?"

"No! I mean, you only broke my heart and left me for another man at dinner, why would it feel awkward?" Zac laughed musically but there was a sharpness behind it and guilt twisted in my stomach.

"It's ok, Alice, I'm teasing! My pride recovered. Why don't you join me, unless you have somewhere else to be?"

Zac gestured to the chair on the other side of the table and I hesitantly pulled it out and sat down. I picked up a menu as the scent of Zac's aftershave drifted on the air. He smelt musky, manly and I found myself wondering what his skin would taste like under my tongue.

"Alice?"

"Huh?" Had I been staring at him? I felt my face redden. Zac grinned at me.

"Am I that boring?"

"Sorry, Zac, no, definitely not boring, I was in my own world."

"Anywhere nice?"

I sighed. I couldn't exactly tell him the truth so instead I said, "I've just left a client meeting rather abruptly and I don't know if I made a massive mistake or not." I regaled the story of my four-hour meeting. Zac looked impressed.

"Well," he said, waving at the waiter, "I'll be surprised if they don't give you the work, that was a ballsy move."

"It was a little mans-club, I'm not so sure."

We placed our order with the waiter and chatted amiably with each other. He had always been easy to talk to and that hadn't changed, and, of course, he was definitely easy to look at. I didn't want to compare him to Lucien, but they were so very different it was hard not to. I wanted to ask Zac about his life, mainly because I was curious about a love interest, but it felt as though it would be for the wrong reasons.

It would make me feel jealous.

It shouldn't, I'd made my choice and despite the occasional ups and downs, I was happy with my choice but the longer I sat with Zac the more I began to imagine a life with him, and for the first time since I'd met Lucien, I was tempted.

Lunch passed in a blur. I know I was engaging, he laughed at my jokes and the conversation flowed comfortably, but at times I was a shell and my mind was going to places it should never have gone. It was both a relief and a disappointment when the waiter brought the bill over.

"Do you want a lift back to the office?" Zac asked.

"I'm not sure I'm dressed for the back of a bike!" I gestured to my skirt. "I'd end up flashing London and I'm not sure they're ready for that!"

"You'll be fine. It'll save you the tube at this time of day."

I glanced at my watch. "Bloody hell, it's later than I'd thought."

"Come on, Alice. You may like being a biker chick!"

I laughed. "God help me!"

***

It was inevitable that Lucien would be glowering from the doorstep of the office when I roared up with Zac. The bike ride through London had been exhilarating and I'm pretty sure I screamed on a few occasions which just made Zac go faster. I clamoured inelegantly from the pillion and Zac parked the bike.

"I'll go up and see Saffron," he said, "if that's ok?"

"Yeah, please do. Although you'll have to excuse the mess, we've only just moved in. We're on the top floor."

"Mr Ross." Zac said nodding curtly at Lucien. Lucien stood blocking the doorway. "If you'll excuse me?"

Lucien continued to stand in the way, flashing a dark look at me. I felt my heart sink. "Lucien, Zac is going to see Saffron, can you let him past please." Lucien slowly moved to one side, enough that Zac could pass him, but not enough to prevent contact between the two. Lucien had height on his side and a body hardened with years of gym work, but Zac had the brutal strength of a soldier. There was a slam of shoulder bones as they came into contact. Lucien said nothing, just stared at me, his features masked with an anger that radiated from him. It enveloped me and I felt the thickness weigh heavy on my limbs until they refused to move.

I shifted, just enough to release tension in my legs. Lucien's stance changed and he stood, legs apart and arms crossed in front of him as he glared at me. If it was to intimidate me, it worked. If he was going to get away with the intention to dominate me, he could think again. With a deep breath in I walked towards him, willing my

76

leaden body to cooperate. It had been a long time since Lucien had made me feel like this, but he wasn't going to get away with it.

I'd done nothing wrong.

"That looked cosy." He sneered as I reached him. "Anything you'd like to tell me."

"Not particularly." I said, my haughty tone hiding the quiver in my voice.

"I wondered why you'd been gone all day, now I know. Exciting was it?"

"Get over yourself, Lucien, and grow up a bit, will you?" I pushed past him and hurried across the marble floor to the lift. He wasn't far behind me but thankfully the lift door closed before he reached me and took me to the sanctuary of the top floor.

LUCIEN

I wanted to storm up to Alice's office and throw Zac fucking Eaton out of my building, but to do so would no doubt give him a power I didn't want him to have. It was excruciating to see Alice climbing from the back of his motorbike, exhilaration in her eyes, looking dishevelled and sexy. Her skirt was tucked up around the tops of her thighs, with her little lacy panties on show, panties that I'd bought her, panties that her fucking khaki-wearing hero had no doubt copped an eye full of as he drove her back.

Fuck, I was pissed.

Seriously pissed.

I walked back into the building and headed to the gym. The only way I would be able to calm the jealous rage that was engulfing me was to push my body to breaking point. I needed the burn. I actually needed to fuck Alice, but she was upstairs fluttering her eyelashes at the soldier who had reappeared out of the fucking blue. The more fucked off I felt, the more my scar pulled on my cheek and when I rubbed it, it felt hot, too hot to touch. Would I ever be free?

The gym was full of staff who'd finished work for the day. I nodded at some of them and headed for the changing room. I kept five sets of gym kit in my locker, one for each day of the week and I grabbed one and quickly changed. When I went back out onto the gym floor, some of the scantily clad girls began flexing, it wasn't unpleasant to see them preening and it flattered my ego that they were doing it for me.

I did some stretches in front of the mirror and moved to the free weights, selecting the ones that would bring the most pain to my muscles. The girls pretended they weren't watching but I could see their eyes flick over to me each time I raised the weights above my head. *It's not just you who can play this game, Alice.*

I wondered how John Frank was getting on. He would have arrived in Zurich by now, but his plans once there hadn't yet been finalised. Carol had booked his hotel and he had access to an unlimited expense account, but as to how he managed his search, well that all depended on what he uncovered. It had been all I'd thought about all day and Alice not being around had made things feel long and drawn out. It was worse that I knew she'd been with Zac. Even worse was that I didn't know why she had been with him. Had it been pre-planned?

I selected another set of weights, ones too heavy ordinarily, but I took the strain and lifted them. The veins in my arms pulsed and my heart beat out a new rhythm as I did the reps. One of the gym employees, Matt, walked past and commented.

"That looks too heavy, Lucien. You may want to tone it down."

"Not today." I puffed out.

"Just be careful."

"It's not in my nature to be anything but." Matt watched me complete a couple of reps and moved to adjust my movements.

"Not too many." He warned and left me to it. I stopped when I saw spots in front of my eyes. The weights had served their purpose, my body was on fire, but I'd not done enough to forget Zac Eaton was in my building.

"Fucker." I hissed under my breath. I walked to the internal phone and dialled Carol.

"Yes Mr Ross?"

"Carol, can you go up to Alice and see if her visitor is still here please? Ring me back on this extension." I hung up and stretched out my aching muscles.

***

"I've come down to say good night." Alice said, shrugging into her jacket.

"Fine."

"Fine? Is that all you're going to say? Not, have a good evening or, do you have anything planned, or even, how was your meeting?"

"I couldn't give a fuck!" I retorted. I was on the stair climber when Alice came into the gym, pushing myself so hard I was headed for a stroke.

"Oh my God, you're such a dick." She exclaimed loudly. Her friends, Clare and Bonnie turned from the running machines to look at us, interest on their faces. "Is this because of Zac?"

"Should it be?"

79

"No."

"No? Really? Because he looked pretty pleased with himself when he brought you back."

"I bumped into him, Lucien. Purely by chance, after my meeting."

"How nice for you."

"It was, actually. It was nice to see him." Alice paused and then said, "Although a very different catch up than you have with your old flames, Lucien. In your case, they're usually half naked with their vaginas on show…Good night."

Alice marched from the gym. Clare and Bonnie looked at me with ill-disguised glee at the snippet of conversation and with some strange telepathy immediately stopped what they were doing and ran after Alice

Fuck, fuck, fuck. This was not how today should have gone. Then I noticed the missed call from John on the mobile phone in front of me. Fuck.

ALICE

"I bet you have great make up sex." Bonnie commented handing me a bag of crisps and a glass of wine. "I mean, he smoulders and broods so well I bet he's a demon between the sheets."

"Bonnie! Please." I said, coughing as the wine hit the back of my throat. "That's my boyfriend you're drooling over."

"She has to drool over him, Alice." Clare said pushing her sweaty hair back from her face. "She's still shagging Billy the Sandwich Man don't forget, and he couldn't brood his way out of a sandwich bag!"

"Why did I see hot Zac in the office? Was he there to see you?"

"I bumped into him after my meeting. He was in a bar that I went into to get some lunch and so I sat with him and had lunch. It was nice to catch up, then he gave me a lift back to work and went up to see Saffron. Obviously, Lucien read more into it and now I'm here with you two gossips."

"Cue the hot make up sex." Bonnie said looking glum. "Billy is an animal between the sheets, as I'm sure I've told you on a few occasions, but we don't argue, ever, so there is none of that intense shagging that comes after a good argument."

"Arguments aren't always good though, Bonnie." I said thoughtfully. "It's not great for the soul. Every time Lucien and I argue, my stomach twists and I want to vomit. Like now, I know he's pissed off with me, he jumped to conclusions about Zac but having been on the end of an old flame blatantly trying it on with Lucien, I know how he is feeling. The fact that he doesn't trust me is a real fucker, but I get it. I also know he has a lot going on, and me arriving at the office on the back of Zac's bike would not have helped. There won't be any make up sex for me today."

"Let's get drunk then!" Clare said brandishing the wine. "I've been to the gym, I burnt a shit load of calories watching Lucien, I've earned this!"

"You two get drunk," I said, "with my blessing. I have a to-do list that isn't going down and I spent half of today in a meeting that was probably a complete waste of time, and the other half having lunch with someone I dated once. Not the best use of my day."

81

"Not the worse use either. At least the bloke you used to date was hot. I've practically dried up. I can't remember the last time I got laid, honestly I'm almost a born again virgin." Clare moaned. "I'd even have a one-night stand with the chubby male cleaner if it got my bits working!"

"You're gross." Bonnie said, pulling a face. "He makes Billy look like Chris Hemsworth."

"You're grasping…"

"A girl can wish!" Bonnie sighed. "I mean, Billy is great in bed but he's not forever man, I can't have wedding photos with his face on them, he's just not pretty. It depresses me because I'm twenty-nine and I'm still at fuck-buddy stage and there has to be more for me, surely?"

There was a depressed sigh around the table and a strange silence until Lucien appeared beside us looking furious.

"Alice." He said, his tone dark and sinister.

Bonnie and Clare looked between him and me, Clare chewing her lip with a grimace on her face while we waited for him to say something. It was clear from his stance and the way he said my name, that he was more pissed off than I'd considered. Bonnie's eyebrows disappeared into her hairline as I calmly picked up my glass. I wasn't calm, I was never calm when Lucien was uber-raging but at least the shaking was inside my body, not in the hand that held the glass.

"Hello Lucien." I said, smiling sweetly. "Are you joining us?"

"No."

"Were you meant to be picking me up?" I looked at my watch knowing full well that nothing had been arranged for the evening. As it was, my trip to the bar was an impromptu reaction to our cross words in the gym earlier. "I don't recall."

"We're going now." Lucien snapped.

"Uh, no, *we're* not. You may be going, but I have a drink and actually, I'm not ready to leave."

Lucien glowered at me and I felt my inside shrink under the ferocity of his glare. He started to say something and instead, turned sharply and stormed out of the bar, knocking a barman who spilt a tray of drinks all over a customer he was serving. Lucien made no acknowledgement as he left.

"Well...shit!" Clare said, "I knew he could do mean and moody but fuck me, he does an impressively smoking-hot brood. You're so lucky, you're going to end up having the best sex of your life."

"Oh please." I said, shrugging nonchalantly. I wasn't nonchalant, my stomach had fallen through the floor and was on its way to the other side of the world, but I wasn't going to be anything other than outwardly in control. *Fuck, fuckity, fuck, fuck, fuck.* "It'll all blow over, Lucien has been known to overreact!"

Neither Bonnie nor Clare looked convinced, but we ordered another bottle of wine which was nothing more than a ploy, by me, to delay the inevitable.

***

I'd half expected Lucien to be waiting for me, simmering, when I got home but there was no angry man on my doorstep, nor was there any messages on my phones or email. I unlocked my front door and pushed it open, stopping to pick up a thick white envelope on the mat.

Anxiety crept into my stomach, knotting and kneading until I felt sick. He had been mad at me before, but never silent with it.

Had I played it wrong?

I slammed the door behind me and dropped my keys onto the table. The silence in my flat was unnerving for a change so I flicked on the TV and left it running while I poured a glass of water and opened the envelope.

It was a white, frothy - that's the only way it could be described - invitation to Xander and Hugo's wedding with a smaller invitation to be Xander's Best Woman. I was so happy for Xander to have found Hugo, the acceptance of his parents and a life that he had so desperately needed. Xander had found being gay a burden in the beginning, fearful of rejection from high society because of the choices he had been born to make. I watched him sleep around London, looking for that special someone who would make it all feel right, and he did. Finally. And he deserved that love, Xander was one of life's best people, kind, funny and generous to a fault. If it hadn't been for Xander, Addison Graphics would never have made it into existence. I owed him so much.

I pushed the call button my mobile and waited for Xander to answer.

"So, someone is actually making an honest man of you?" I grinned down the phone. "It's about time."

"Isn't it the most revolting, meringue-like invite you've ever seen?" He said grumpily. "Bloody Hugo's bloody mother chose it because it was like the one her Grandmother had from some closest gay in the Royal family from way back when. I wanted chic. I got chinz."

I laughed. "It's not really you but, I don't know Xan, I kinda like it, it's very 'gay wedding!'"

"It's an invite fit for a raging bloody queen. We're not queens we're stylish gays!"

"Yes, you are…"

"Honestly, Alice, what will people think?"

"Maybe they'll just think they'll be attending the wedding of two very special people? No one keeps the invites anyway."

"That's easy for you to say, Alice, it's not your wedding invite that looks like a bloody nineteen-eighties bed ruffle. They all got hand delivered today by a courier, so there was no chance I could accidentally drop them into the Thames and get some new ones done."

"Xander?" I asked gently. "Is this more to do with pre-wedding nerves than the invitations?"

"Maybe." Xander replied in a small voice. "Maybe I'm scared."

"Why?"

"Because fabulous things like Hugo don't happen to people like me. You know that, Alice. You've seen how I behaved. You know me better than anyone, and after all the one night stands and broken hearts, how has this happened? With someone like him, I mean? He's amazing and gorgeous and so sexy I drool every time I look at him. I have more hang-ups than Marks and sodding Spencer…"

"Xan?" I said softly.

"What?"

"You need to take a deep breath."

"Why?"

"You are the most special person in the world, you've been my knight in shining armour on more occasions than I could count and honestly, Xander, I'd be completely lost without you. You deserve this happiness more than anyone I know, because you have a heart of gold and because it's your turn. I will be so proud to stand beside you and watch you marry the love of your life, and who cares if the invites have brought the eighties back, it's not important, not compared to the wedding and your life afterwards…and besides, it's always something to show the kids."

"What if no one will surrogate for us?" Xander was grasping at all his insecurities.

"If a supermodel won't donate, you can have one of my eggs…"

"I love you, Alice you're a wonderful friend and if Bella Hadid isn't available then…"

"Bella Hadid? I take it you didn't have short and round on your maternal wish list?"

"You're not round, more…soft!"

"I'm so glad I rang you, Xan. I'm now thinking the frothy invites was karma foreseeing this conversation!" I laughed heartily. I know he and Hugo would have my egg in a heartbeat, if I wanted to give it away. Xander and I had had plenty of drunken conversations about producing a child together but, if I was honest, when I imagined children, it was as part of a loving relationship, not a turkey-baster moment in Kensington. I saw children in my future, little bundles of joy that looked like Lucien… Fuck.

"How's your hot man, anyway, you've not mentioned him once in this conversation." Xander said. "Still having epic sex?"

"We're not speaking."

"Why not?"

"I had an unplanned lunch and ride back to the office with Zac, Lucien didn't like it…"

"The soldier? Is he still as handsome as fuck?"

"Yep, very much so. It was a very easy lunch, was awkward to begin with after everything, not really surprising, but once that was all out of the way, it was really nice to see him. Lucien, however, didn't think it was very nice…"

"I get that."

"Yeah, so do I, but now we're not speaking, or at least, I assume we're not speaking. We had a row in the office gym and then I was a little dismissive when he came into the bar that I was in…"

"A little?"

"A lot." I admitted.

"Oh."

"Exactly." I sighed and said, "sometimes I just want to feel like I'm the one in control, only it never seems to turn out like it."

"Does he do the controlling then?" Xander's voice hardened. "Because, that's not ok, Alice."

"Oh no, Xander, nothing like you're thinking, God no. I'm still my own person, it's just that sometimes I want to rebel a little, maybe because I worry about my feelings for him, they're so intense and he knows that. I know how he feels about me, and normally all is good and calm, but we've had a few moments recently that just feels like I can't see me. That's all. Nothing sinister…"

"So, he's not being all *domestic abuser* then?"

"No! Definitely not!"

"That's ok then. Phew, I didn't want to have to go around there and beat him to a pulp!" Xander laughed. "Hugo is home, I'm going now. Don't forget to RSVP! You also have to decide what to wear in the colour scheme the wedding planner has chosen, I'll drop it off this week, you can pick whatever you want but I'm sorry Alice, it's really not the right colour for you, but never mind."

I had a sudden vision of walking down the aisle with Xander in a peach puffy ballgown and shuddered. "You're scaring me, can't I wear a suit?"

"God no, his Great Aunt Beatrice will think you're ripe for the taking!"

"Beatrice?"

"She puts the B in butch! Love you."

"Love you." I ended the call and flipped my phone onto the sofa. I sat down heavily. Not the day I'd planned. In my head, this morning, I was winning the contract, taking Saffron out for a celebratory cocktail and spending the evening in bed, or wherever, with Lucien. Now I was in an empty flat having had lunch with my ex-date, drinks with the biggest gossips in the office and walked out of the bid, with visions of peach polyester - yep, a fuck up of a day.

I deliberated phoning Lucien but with no idea of the reception I'd get, I took myself off to bed and willed sleep to come.

LUCIEN

It was him, without a doubt. Jean-Claude, my best friend. The photo John had sent to me was grainy and blurry from the phone camera being zoomed in, but there was no mistaking the face I'd have recognised anywhere. Looking at him brought back a swarm of memories that I felt as though I was being eaten alive by images of the past.

My muscles ached from my hard work out, but they cramped and tensed the longer I held the phone awkwardly in my hand, staring at the picture. Had he and Isabelle always planned to be together? Would she have left me anyway, even if Ottie hadn't died? The endless questions zoomed around, visible in the air as I tried to make sense of the little information I had. Jean-Claude and Isabelle. My best friend and my wife. Had there been an affair? I didn't see any signs but then I never looked. Why would I? I thought the problems we were having was because I was away so much but that summer, we were so close. Did I imagine that? I didn't think so, Isabelle admitted that things had been better. Did I drive her to him? Did he always want Isabelle and used me being away to take her?

I sat down tiredly on the sofa and squeezed my eyes shut, pinching the bridge of my nose to calm the headache that was worsening. I had no answers to the questions, and they would drive me mad if I let them continue to fight for space in my worn-out brain. I needed Alice. She would make sense of things, she always did, but I was so pissed at her, pissed that she would be so casual about having lunch with Zac. Jealousy had never really been one of my faults, I tended to use it to spur myself on in business, rather than love affairs that I had avoided. Until Alice.

I could hear the whiskey bottle on the kitchen counter begin calling my name. It had numbed me over the years, shutting the demons away for a brief moment, but since the day Alice came back in my life, I'd barely touched it. I was fearful of losing her and becoming like my dad, a revolting piss-smelling alcoholic who drank everything he earned and left my mum trying to feed us on what was left. I would never be like him, yet I'd come close. Too many times.

I stood up and crossed to the kitchen, poured the bottle of whiskey down the sink and, grabbing my car keys, left the apartment. I knew where I would find my solace, I was just fearful that someone had jumped in my place.

***

I pressed the buzzer over and over until the sleepy voice answered.

"Hello?"

"It's me."

"Hi you." Alice said, her voice thick with sleep. "Are you coming up?"

"No, can you come down?" I asked her. "Please."

I heard her take a hesitant breath in and the intercom clicked off. The stairwell light came on and through the frosted glass I saw Alice walk down the stairs. From the way she moved I knew she was expecting the worst. The car idled beside me, filling the almost silent air with a low hum as the night sky began to throw down small droplets of rain.

"Hi." Alice said, pulling her dressing gown around herself. "It's the middle of the night, are you ok?"

"Why did you have lunch with him Alice?" I hadn't planned to ask her that, the reason I was on her doorstep was to make some sense of the muddle in my head over Jean-Claude, but the words came out before I could stop them.

"It wasn't planned, Lucien. If it had been planned, I would have told you I was seeing him. I left my awful meeting and was hungry. Zac happened to be in the same restaurant, we sat together. That's all. Nothing sinister, just lunch."

I said nothing. The rain began to fall a little harder and the drops pinged against my face. "Why did you try and show me up in the gym?"

Alice shifted uncomfortably and chewed on her lip. Her arms instinctively wrapped themselves around her middle. "I was annoyed. You jumped to a conclusion and assumed the worst of me. Which was an audacity given the undressed state of Delphine when

89

she was having a supposed meeting with you. I wasn't expecting to come face to face with her vagina when I walked into your office, Lucien, and you were getting stroppy about lunch. It fucked me off, if I'm honest."

"Alice…"

She held her hand up. "You thought it was your right to get shitty about Zac, with whom I shared one or two kisses… Delphine and you got up to all sorts once, why was it ok for her to be in your office with her 'everything' hanging out and not ok for Zac to give me a lift back to the office? Don't you think that that smacks of double standards?"

"I was jealous…"

"Jealous? Really? After everything? It's a little ridiculous, Lucien. Do you not think that me knowing Delphine had been half naked in your office irked a little more? I mean, who knows what you two had been up to, she could have sat there doing a *Basic Instinct* on you for all I knew."

Alice was too close to the mark and I was glad it was dark otherwise she would have seen the guilty flush spread over my face. I rubbed my scar and screwed up my face to release the tightness in it.

"I didn't come here to argue with you."

"I'm not arguing." She said quickly. "It's the middle of the night and I'm too tired to argue, but I'm not going to put up with your shit, Lucien, when most of the time you do worse than me anyway." Alice paused and sucked in a loud breath. "Did you really wake me up to talk about Zac?"

"No, I didn't. I don't really know why I mentioned him. I came over because John has found Jean-Claude and my head feels fucked. It's only ever you who can unfuck my head." I said, kicking at a stone on the floor.

"Are you sure it's him? It's been a long time."

"I'm definitely sure. He's changed his name but there is no mistaking the photo. I'd know him anywhere."

"Oh." Alice looked at a loss for words. She shifted from one foot to the other and glanced at me with her brow furrowed. "You don't seem pleased."

"I don't know how I feel about it, Alice. He was my best friend. He and his wife, Clarisse, Isabelle and I made up a foursome, we were inseparable." I shook my head, trying to rid my mind of the flash of memories. "And now, I'm questioning everything, the past as I knew it, the past decade...I don't know what's real. I don't know if he and Isabelle were having an affair or if their relationship is new. If it was an affair, what does that do to the friendship I thought I had? He put me back together, Alice, rebuilt all the broken bits after the crash. He changed the medical records to prevent me going to jail for drink driving when Ottie died. I don't know how I feel anymore."

I longed for Alice to wrap her arms around me like she always did when I talked about Ottie. It was her understanding that got me through each day, the kindness she showed and the faith she had in me. She didn't move towards me like I'd hoped, instead crossed her arms in front of her and kept her eyes focused on the ground.

"Alice?"

"I don't know what to say." There was a quiver in her voice and a sadness in the tone.

"Why?"

"Because I feel like I'm going to lose you."

The rain dripped loudly onto the roof of the car as her words hung in the air. Was she going to lose me? It didn't feel that way to me, she was my whole world and I told her often enough. Or I thought I did and yet, in that moment, I couldn't remember when I last said anything to reassure her that I was in it for the long haul, or when I last proffered the *I love you* that I knew she needed. Had I already begun to push her away again? Was I protecting her by doing so, or myself? Was that why I let Delphine turn me on?

I did love Alice. I loved her more than I had the words to express but my head was in Switzerland and my mind was questioning my past. I thought I had moved forward, but I was lost in the events that defined me and I was too far from her reach.

"You're not." It sounded weak, feeble almost and from her stance I knew she didn't believe me. I wasn't sure I believed me.

"You could have tried to sound convincing." She said with a tight smile. Alice hunched up her shoulder again the rain and continued, "I thought today felt strange, when I woke up the air felt odd and everything I've done today has felt like a battle. You and I shouldn't feel like a battle, not anymore. I've never wanted anything more for you than you to find your family, and for you to know what really happened. I have never believed that you killed Ottie and to watch you beat yourself up over something you were told, that's been horrific." She shook her head slowly from left to right. "All those nights you woke me up with your screaming, no one should ever have to face those kinds of demons, Lucien. Until you find Hettie and find out the truth, they won't set you free." Alice let go of her dressing gown and reached for my hand. Hers was icy cold and trembling. "I think you need to go to Switzerland."

"What about you?"

"All I can do right now is give you my blessing, Lucien. I'm setting you free."

"Free?"

"Yes." Her voice sounded strangled and I knew the sacrifice she was making was the absolute definition of her love for me. I didn't want to be free of her, life without Alice in it was no life, but she was right, the demons wouldn't let me go until I knew for sure. Finding Hettie had been my focus for the past ten years and now I was closer than ever. I was terrified by what I would find in Switzerland and what John would uncover before I got there. I wanted Hettie to be happy, to feel secure and to have a life full of joy, and maybe it was selfish of me to disrupt the life she had. Perhaps Isabelle was telling the truth when she said Jean-Claude was the only father Henrietta needed.

"It's not a life without you, Alice."

"It's not a life for you if you don't know the truth, Lucien. You have to go, and you can't focus on that if you're worrying about me."

"Is this about him?"

"Who? Zac? No! Zac and I were never anything more than friends, not really."

"You were more than that to him." I said hotly. "So much more."

Alice sighed. "I don't think so, Lucien. It's in your head."

92

I moved closer to her. The rain was harder and biting against my skin. Alice was shivering in her thin dressing gown and an old tee-shirt of mine. My heart pounded a little harder at the sight of beautiful Alice in my clothing. I could smell the scent of her skin being carried by the rain and I breathed it in as deep as I could.

"Come with me?" I whispered. "Please Alice, come with me."

Alice swallowed hard and rubbed her hands over her eyes. "I can't, Lucien. It's not my place."

"Your place is with me." I reached for her and drew her cold body to mine. "I can't do it without you. Only you have ever made the demons go away."

"That's a lot of pressure for a girl," she smiled sadly. "Hettie and Isabelle will take those demons away for good, Lucien. They've always had that power. You have to find the truth and fix things, whatever it is that has to be fixed."

"Don't do this Alice." I said, wrapping my arms around her shoulders and burying my face in her hair. She smelled so good, floral and feminine, a scent that was perfumed just for me. "Please don't do this."

Alice let out the smallest, barely audible sob. "I'm not doing anything permanent, Lucien."

"It feels like it." I said, choking back a pain so extraordinary I'd only felt it once before. "Will you be here when I get back?"

"Yes." Alice whispered, her arms gripped me tightly and her face was wet against my chest, but there was no truth in her voice. I had lost her. My guardian angel was letting me go. "You need to go now, Lucien, otherwise I won't be able to let go."

"Then don't." I said, echoing the same words she used when I was leaving her in Paris. "Be the one I wake up with."

Alice shook her head. "I'd never be able to let you go if I did that. You have to go, Lucien. Go and find Hettie, I'll be waiting."

"For how long?"

Alice reached for my face and cupped my cheeks in her hands. Her palms, usually so warm, were freezing. "Kiss me." She said, not answering my question. "Kiss me like it's forever."

She pulled my face down to hers and my mouth sought out her lips. Tears mingled with the rain as the kiss became more urgent and demanding.

"I love you." I whispered against her mouth and Alice's hands tightened around my face. She didn't want to let go any more than I did but she was right, this was my journey and maybe her insight was spot on – maybe I did have to do this alone.

"I love you." She pulled at my lips with her teeth, gently, but I know what she was doing, she was staking her claim.

The kiss deepened and I lost myself in it. For a moment there was no Switzerland, there was just her and I, until she pulled away and stood back, wrapping her dressing gown tighter around her.

"You need to go now."

"Why?"

"Because if you don't, I won't be able to let you go." Alice choked on a sob. "It doesn't feel like you'll be coming back to me."

"Please don't do this." I begged her. "I know why you are but I need you, I need you with me."

"Not for this, this is your journey. Be safe, Lucien."

"Wait for me?"

"Be safe."

She was gone back inside before my heart took another beat. Had the worst thing just happened, had I just lost Alice?

ALICE

I'd handed myself to the wolves, the ones who circled my bed, snapping and snarling all night. I'd heard Lucien's car pull away, sloshing tyres in the rain that had turned heavy and I wrapped myself up in my duvet and lay staring blankly into the blackness.

What had I done?

I hadn't planned this. I hadn't planned to let him go nor feel so sure it was the right thing. I was holding him back and my fear was that his search for his family would be affected by his feelings for me. Our relationship had been so up and down recently with endless drama that I felt certain I would somehow stop him giving his all to the search. He had to find Hettie and he had to know the truth and he couldn't do that in London with me.

I'd set him free, but I had no idea if he would come back to me.

I couldn't imagine my life without Lucien in it. Not waking up and him being the first thing I saw, not feeling his arms around me or his crushing kisses or the deviance that he had shown me in the bedroom. Anguish twisted my gut until I dry retched over the side of the bed. This was agony and it was my doing. I could have gone with him, but I chose not to, and I wondered if it was more about me, self-preservation to keep him from breaking my heart again – let him go before he did it to me.

Paris was never far from my thoughts as I lay there in the dark. His words had almost mirrored mine and it felt as though history was repeating itself, only I was breaking my own heart.

I missed him already.

Tomorrow I would be in the office with no idea of what to say when I was asked where he was. I couldn't imagine how it would feel when I walked into the building and know he wasn't there, that he was far away from me looking for the first woman he ever loved. I believed that he loved me, but the bond between him and Isabelle would be unbreakable because of Hettie.

I willed sleep to come, to escape the complexity of my thoughts and to prevent the unending tears that fell, soaking my pillow. Eventually, when there were no tears left, I fell into a restless sleep and when I woke, the emptiness felt like a personality in the room.

Fuck.
Had he really gone?

LUCIEN

The start of our working relationship may have been the stuff of nightmares, but in recent months Carol had proved herself to be worth so much more than her weight in gold. She pre-empted everything well in advance of me actually needing it, and that morning had been no exception. Within an hour she had a private jet on standby, a hotel reservation and all my meetings rescheduled.

I had no idea what I would find in Switzerland and going without Alice meant my demons would certainly follow me there. They taunted me during the long night and as I boarded the plane, I could hear their vicious taunts. Fuck.

My scar burned. It had been getting hotter and hotter over recent weeks but as I sat in my seat, the pain was almost as intense as the day I got it. Eventually I wrapped some ice in a napkin, held it to my cheek and waited for the flight to be over. It was a short flight, but it seemed to drag on and on. I had my laptop open with the idea to send urgent emails, but I found myself staring out of the window, thoughts flicking between Alice and Hettie so quickly it made me feel dizzy.

A car was waiting at the airport for me and I was driven quickly to my hotel in Zurich. I paid the city no attention as I sat jigging my legs up and down wondering what John would have for me. I could barely breathe as the enormity of the trip hit me with a tsunamic force from all sides. What the fuck was I doing? I scratched my scar which felt red hot under my fingertips, and took a few deep breaths in. The playmates would all laugh if they could see the great Lucien Ross - controlling, dominant, powerful Lucien Ross, award winning businessman with a multi-million-pound empire – about to crumble into a monumental panic attack.

I fumbled in my pocket, willing my hands to work properly, and pulled out my phone, dropping it with a clatter onto my laptop bag. "Shit."

Dialling the number, I took some steadying breathes and waited for the answer.

"Lucien? Is everything alright?" Alice sounded flustered, as though I'd crossed the line.

"No." I whispered, holding my palm against my burning scar and feeling a prickling behind my eyes. It had been years since I'd cried or given into emotions that weren't brought on by excesses of whiskey, but sitting in the car, on my own, with my love so far away, suddenly the shackles of my past tightened unbearably and I saw black spots dance in front of my eyes. Shit, I was going to pass out.

"Lucien? Lucien?" Alice's voice rang with concern. I couldn't make my mouth work to answer her and beads of sweat began to cover my forehead. My scar felt as though it was ripping open and splitting my eyeball with a fire that burned so hot it was almost icy. I couldn't breathe.

"Lucien, for fuck's sake, speak to me. Lucien? Shit. Lucien?" I could hear her talking to someone, Saffron I supposed, and then her voice down the phone said, "Lucien, will you please say something?"

I wanted to talk, I wanted to tell her it was all ok and that I was the control freak I always was, but my tongue was swollen in my mouth and had slowly begun to choke me.   I   made   a   strange gagging sound and Alice's voice went up an octave.

"Lucien? For fuck's sake Lucien, you're scaring me, will you fucking speak." I could hear the panic in her voice and longed to reassure but the words would not come. "Lucien? Shit, Saffron find out where he is, fuck, Lucien?" I hung up the phone and tossed it onto the seat.

"Sir?" The driver said, glancing up at me in the rear-view mirror. Fuck knows what he must have thought when he saw me pale and clammy. "We are here."

He pulled up outside the reception and a suited doorman opened my door. I picked up my phone and laptop bag and exited the car clumsily - there was no refinement in my movements at all. My legs were leaden as I followed the doorman into the air-conditioned hotel foyer. Had it been a different trip, I would have been very impressed with the hotel that Carol had booked for me at really short notice, but on that day, it felt like I was walking into a prison for a lifetime in solitary confinement.

I could feel my phone vibrating in my pocket and I knew it was probably Alice. I should have answered, my earlier contact with her would have made her fearful. She'd been at the end of my meltdowns more times than she should have. For now, it was easier to focus on the mundane task of checking in, than it was talking to her.

I missed her.

Fuck, I loved her.

She had put up with me and stood by me and had an unwavering faith in me, yet at that moment, where I was feeling at my most vulnerable, she may as well have shouted 'Red' at me and walked away.

I needed her here, yet she set me free.

Fuck, I needed a drink.

ALICE

The fear was all too familiar. A broken Lucien, unreachable due to the demons who wouldn't let him go. I hated them. Hated the voices that whispered to him in the middle night causing him to scream out in terror. Knowing he was in Switzerland all alone, save for the PI that he employed, and realising I'd made a massive mistake nearly ripped my guts out through my throat. I doubled up and a strange sound erupted from me prompting Saffron to rush across the office to keep me up.

"Shit, shit, fucking shit, Alice, what's the matter?"

"I have to go."

"Go where? What's happened with Lucien? Where is he? Is he ill?"

I shut my eyes tightly to stop the world from swimming. "It's too long to explain, Saffron." The breaths I took in did nothing to quell the nausea. "I have to go and see Carol."

"Why?"

"Because I need her to book me onto a flight. Today."

"What? What about work?"

"This is more important Saff." The phone rang and she looked from me to the phone.

"Do you want me to get that?"

"Yes please." I waited until she'd answered the phone before I took the lift down to Lucien's office. I could smell his scent in the corridor as I walked along to Carol's desk and it made the longing to be with him worse. I should never have said what I did, I should have realised that he would have needed me with him. He'd needed me at every stage of this painful process, from visiting Ottie's grave to picking him up when he fell under the weight of his past. Shit, what had I been thinking to have abandoned him?

I thought it had been the right thing, that it would have been better for him to focus on his family, not worrying about me, but I had been completely wrong. Fuck, how had I got it so wrong?

"Hi Alice." Carol said smiling up at me. She was good for Lucien, she took none of his shit and her quiet demeanour calmed him. She had had a wobbly start with Lucien, having to put up with his mood swings and his near-descent into a unmanageable whisky habit, but they now had a good working relationship and he depended on her.

"Hi Carol. I need your help."

"Oh?" Carol stopped typing and looking questioningly at me.

"I need you to get me on a plane to Zurich as soon as possible."

Carol's face fell. "I take it this trip hasn't gone to plan?"

"How much do you know?" I asked her.

Carol sighed. "Probably more than I should. I hear him sometimes on the phone and I've seen adoption papers that he hadn't meant for me to have, but they ended up piled with work documents. Not that I read them," she said quickly. "But I saw the name and have put two and two together."

I sighed. "Then you know almost all of it. I have to get there today. I don't care what it costs, the company can pick up the bill, but please Carol, you know where he's staying. Please get me there."

Carol picked up the phone. "Leave it with me, I'll come up as soon as I have you on a flight."

"Thank you." I smiled tightly at her and left the office, walking back to the lift.

Saffron was waiting for me when I got back upstairs. "I'm not sure if this is going to please you," she said, "but you won the bid you went for last week. According to the man I spoke to, your ballsy attitude was more impressive than your price!"

"Oh crap." I sat down heavily. "This is absolutely the wrong time for a new client. I have to go to Zurich today."

"Well," Saffron commented, "you'll have to take your laptop with you because you cannot turn down that money."

"You're so bossy."

"I know, that's why you've employed me when no one else has!" Saffron laughed. "Seriously though Alice, you cannot turn that work down, the market is slowing, it's a turbulent time out there and you need to protect yourself if the supposed recession hits."

"Do I? How do you know all this?"

"I may look like dumb, but I do read!" Saffron looked affronted. "Unlike you who seems to drift around on a wave of Lucien love, I

101

keep an eye on the wellbeing of the country, to see if I need to relocate somewhere more stable. And, I'm telling you Alice, you need to make sure the bank is full, because tough times are coming."

"Ok!" I smiled, "I'll take my laptop and start work as soon as I get to the airport. Have they sent the full spec?"

"Not yet, it's being couriered over, so you can't go anywhere until it arrives."

"I may have to."

"Seriously Alice…"

Saffron's rant was cut short by Carol rushing into the office.

"Alice, I've got a plane on standby. I need you to sign off the expense because, honestly, if Lucien goes nuts…"

"It's fine, Carol." I said taking the expense docket from her. "And if it's not, I'll deal with it. You can always tell Lucien I held a bat to your head!" I signed the document and balked at the price. "It's just as well Lucien is loaded," I muttered feeling my face pale at the sight of the zeros. "I'm going to the airport…"

"You haven't packed!" Saffron said.

"It's ok, they have shops in Zurich. Thanks Carol, you're a star. Saffron can you scan and email the documents to me when they arrive. Make something up if anyone calls, tell them someone died or something, and keep me updated. I'll work on the plane to get the Montell brief ready, you can send it onto them later. It'll be fine." Neither Carol or Saffron looked convinced. "Trust me." I shoved my laptop, tablet, phone and notebook into my bag, hugged Saffron, kissed Carol on the cheek and ran down the stairs and into a waiting cab.

All I could hope was that Lucien was in one metaphorical piece when I arrived.

LUCIEN

John Frank was waiting for me in the hotel lounge. When he saw me walk in, he signalled to the waitress who brought over a tray with two glasses of whiskey and a cafetière of coffee. I sat down and nodded at her, picking up the whiskey and recoiling at the smell.

"Just coffee." I said to her, putting the whiskey back down, and she leaned forward to pour the coffee into my cup. "Thanks."

John picked up his whiskey glass and took a sip. "Not like you to turn down Scotland's finest."

I shrugged. "So, what do you know? Is Isabelle here? And Hettie?"

"I've not seen Hettie, but Isabelle is here. She frequents a small coffee shop in town, most mornings. I've followed her in there once or twice."

"And?" My heart thudded painfully against my ribs.

"And she has expresso, a croissant sometimes, other times brioche toast, nothing unusual for a woman alone. She talks on her phone, reads the paper, normal things like that. It's always around nine, I guess if Henrietta is here, she'll be in school."

"She must be here, Isabelle wouldn't leave her anywhere, she has no family...well none that she speaks to."

"That you know of." John said. "I've kept my following to a very safe distance so I don't have all the gaps filled and I've not seen Hettie but Isabelle spends most of her time alone, sometimes she goes to the gym and I see her with a couple of women, mainly for lunch at a restaurant nearby. I've not gone as far as to follow her home, but I've been following Jean-Claude, casually, keeping my distance."

"You know where he is?" It wasn't really a question. I reached for the whiskey in front of me and took a long drink, nearly downing the measure. I wiped my mouth on a napkin.

"He works at the hospital. I asked the reception about him, using my usual line of questions that has everyone giving me the answers I want. He splits his time being the lead Surgeon at the city hospital and working as a consultant at the psychiatric unit."

"He didn't work in psychiatry, I guess things really do change."

"I checked his credentials and he isn't qualified, I can't even find any proof he's being paid, so maybe he's volunteering there, although it's a ludicrously expensive unit. It seems that only the very wealthy can be crackpots in this town."

"Anything else?"

"He gets to work at eight am, leaves around six, goes to the gym, has a drink after and gets a car home around eight. It's a chauffeur driven car, I guess even the sick in this town are wealthy."

"He comes from money."

"But I haven't yet found out where Henrietta is."

I felt my heart sink.

"I will, Lucien. She has to be here, it's just a question of tracking them. Give me time."

"I will be here with you. I'm not going back to London until I find her. Not now I'm this close."

"You look like shit, if you don't mind me saying so." John commented, not unkindly.

"I can't say I feel too great either, mate." My hands shook as I reached for the whisky glass. "I have to find her, John. She has to be here somewhere because Isabelle would have her somewhere safe, she knows I've been looking for them so she wouldn't make it easy. It's probably why Jean-Claude changed his name. Shady fucker."

I felt such a rage that my hand clenched into a fist, so tight that my skin went almost translucent. He was my best friend and he stole my life. I wanted to kill him.

"Do you need a large one?" John nodded at the empty glass.

"No." I shook my head and reached for my coffee. "I got dragged out of that mess, I'm not going back. So, what do we do now?"

"The next step is to find where they live and see if Hettie is there. I'll do that, I've hired a van, it's less suspect than a car..."

"I'll come with you."

John shook his head. "You could blow it, Lucien. It's taken this long, he's changed his name, the last thing we want is for them to run somewhere and we have to start again. It's happened to me before, when a client gets involved, it all goes to shit. This has been a ten-year project. Let me handle it."

He was right, of course. John had worked for me for years, dug me out of holes, tracked down all sorts of undesirables who owed me money, and always got me answers when I needed them. Isabelle had been the one case he couldn't ever seem to crack, she had always been one step ahead, moving from place to place until she had vanished completely. Now I was closer than I'd ever been and there was no way I was screwing it up. Zurich's population was tiny in comparison to London and the risk of bumping into Isabelle or Jean-Claude were too high for comfort.

John drained his drink and wiped his mouth with the napkin on the tray. "Get some rest, Lucien. Leave the shit to me. I've got a team flying in, we'll have this done and dusted in no time. You have my word."

I yawned widely, suddenly feeling exhausted. The panic attack had drained my energy and focus and the need for a long, dreamless sleep was a pull I could not longer avoid.

"Thanks John." I said, standing up and stretching out my shoulders. "I feel fucked, I'm going to my room. Ring me when you know more."

"Will do." John said. I left him to sign for the bill and crossed the lounge to take the lift to my room. I was on the top floor with panoramic views of the city and the river beyond. Somewhere, out there, was my baby girl, and if it was the last thing I did, I would find her.

My life would not be complete until I did.

ALICE

I thought flying back in first class from St Lucia with Lucien had been the most luxurious way to travel but it in no way compared to flying in a private jet. I was welcomed on board by a smiling, suited hostess who handed me a hot hand towel followed by a glass of ice-cold champagne. For a fleeting moment I forgot why I was travelling like that and enjoyed the sheer opulence of being in a sleek, designer-decorated jet.

I barely noticed that we had taken off, there was none of the clanking and clunking of a passenger plane, until I glanced out of the windows at the cotton wool clouds beneath us. The pilot came out and introduced himself once we were at our directed altitude, shaking my hand with a firm grip.

"Are you travelling to Zurich for business or pleasure?" He asked in a smooth, deep voice.

"Neither." I replied, "it's a trip for personal reasons."

"Shame. Zurich is a wonderful city for a break, so much to see."

"I hope to see some of it." I said. "My timetable is open-ended at the moment."

He looked at me with inquisitive eyes. Self-consciously I ran my fingers in a combing motion through my tangled hair. I didn't fit the mould of private jet passenger and I wondered what he thought of my reasons for travelling to Zurich. I shouldn't have cared, but I did.

The pilot excused himself and the stewardess brought over a tray of canapes which I barely touched. I couldn't eat. Every time I thought about Lucien, my stomach twisted with anxiety. I hoped fervently that I was panicking unnecessarily, but the endless unanswered calls and texts made me fearful. I knew how low he could get, and I felt sick that he was struggling there alone.

I should have gone with him.

If anything happened to Lucien, it would be my fault.

It was a short flight to Zurich, but the clock ticked by so slowly it could almost have been going backwards. The champagne did nothing to quell my nerves, despite me nearly drinking a bottle of it. I was as sober getting off the plane as I had been getting on it.

I was escorted from our docking bay by a uniformed airport employee who had me through immigration in record time. A car was waiting for me in the arrivals bay and I sank into the seat suddenly feeling an overpowering wave of emotion wash over me. I was there, I would hold his hand through this, and I would never let him go again.

***

"I'm sorry Miss Addison, I cannot allow you into the suite, you are not booked as a guest here." I wanted to hit the petite, blonde receptionist. She had told me three times already that she would not tell me which room Lucien was in and I could tell her patience was wearing out. I didn't give a shit.

"Mr Ross is expecting me." I insisted again.

The receptionist sighed and gave a small incline of her head to hovering security guard. "Again, Miss Addison, I'm sorry. You are welcome to wait in the lounge until he comes down and I will tell him you're here. That's as much as I can do."

"His PA rang ahead."

"I'm sorry, we have no record of that call. Nor could I even divulge his room to her, we take our guests security very seriously." She beckoned the security guard forward. He was huge, built like a rugby player on steroids. "Please escort Miss Addison to the lounge and ask one of the bar team to take her refreshments."

"Can you at least send someone up to check on his welfare, please?"

"Is Mr Ross in danger?" She looked nervous.

"I am concerned about him. He was unwell when he called me this morning and I want to make sure he's ok. If that's not too much trouble."

"I will ensure a check on Mr Ross is done. Will there be anything else?"

"No. Just that, thank you." I gave her as dark a look as possible which she replied to with a beaming smile.

"It was delightful to have met you Miss Addison and I am sure this will be resolved soon." It didn't sound like she was delighted or hopeful.

I didn't bother to reply just followed the genetically modified man to the lounge where he showed me to a corner table. "I'll have a waitress bring you coffee." He said. His voice was so low it was almost inaudible, just a vibration of deep sound.

"Thanks."

I sat down heavily in the chair feeling exhausted. It had been an emotionally charged morning and sitting in a public lounge wasn't part of my arrival plan. I opened my laptop bag and put the machine on the table. Once I was on the hotel Wi-Fi I logged into my email and stared unenthusiastically at the long list of client demands, bid invites and the new brief from the business we'd just won.

When I won the Young Entrepreneur Award, they said it would change my business, bring an unending stream of new clients to my door and quadruple my turnover. 'They' weren't wrong, but it was wearing me out, I worked all the time, trying to keep up with bids and presentations and ensuring that every client had the very best of me. I wasn't cheap and had no intention of devaluing my work by trying to undercut my peers, but I needed a break at some point, I was losing my focus.

Of course, that focus had been shifted entirely to the person upstairs who I was praying was alright.

"Miss Addison?"

"Yes?" I looked up at the waitress who had brought over a tray of coffee.

"Reception have asked me to tell you that Mr Ross is well, and he is sleeping."

"Oh, thank God."

"Do you need anything else?" She asked.

"No, I'm good here, thank you." The waitress left me alone and I poured out the coffee and turned my attention back to my emails.

LUCIEN

I slept so deeply I woke feeling heavy and lethargic and for a moment had no idea where I was. I glanced at the clock. Fuck, I'd been asleep for hours. Stretching, I forced my aching muscles to move, the pounding from the gym and the tension from recent events had me grimacing as I wriggled up to sitting.

I had complete faith in John but the need to do something was grating on me, now that I was awake. I wanted to help but I also had a fear of hindering John in his work. I pressed the button for the automatic blinds on the panel beside the bed and they began to rise, letting the evening sun in. Zurich was so small, I had to be so careful, one wrong move and Jean-Claude, Isabelle and Hettie could be gone in a flash. We were too close for that.

The phone, on the side table, was flashing so I pressed the message button and listened to the greeting from the front desk.

"Mr Ross, this is Angelique on Reception. A Miss Addison arrived a little while ago and will be waiting in the lounge for you. If this visit isn't expected or welcome, please advise and we will ask her to leave the premises. The wellbeing of our guests is our top priority." The message clicked off and I sat bolt upright. Alice was here? Now? In this hotel? She'd come? *I'm setting you free.* I was so sure she had meant it and now she was here.

I got dressed faster than my sore body appreciated and was in the lift down to the lounge before I'd taken a breath. She knew I needed her, and she'd come, just like every time I'd fallen, she was there to pick me up. Fuck, I loved her, everything about her. She was mine and I was hers and her being here just proved it all the more.

When the lift opened, I hurried through the bar and into the lounge. Alice was there, working on her laptop, a pen in her mouth and a notebook balanced on her knee. She looked tired but more beautiful than I'd ever seen her look.

"Alice?"

"Lucien, thank fuck." She said standing up quickly, the notebook falling from her lap. She took the pen from her mouth and chucked it onto the chair before rushing over to me. "I've been so worried. I thought something terrible had happened." Alice reached up to my

109

face and pulled it down towards her. Kissing my mouth, she pushed her body against mine and whispered, "I'm sorry, I'm so sorry. I thought I was doing the right thing and it was totally the wrong thing. I'm so sorry, Lucien."

I wrapped my arms around her and breathed in the floral scent, feeling my anxiety melting away. "Thank fuck you're here." I said against her neck, "thank fuck." Alice was trembling and I felt a dampness on my shirt. "Don't cry, Alice. Please don't cry."

"I was so scared. When you rang, I thought the worst had happened, and I wasn't here when you needed me to be." She pulled her face from my chest and looked up at me. "And, I owe you several thousand pounds for my flight!" She grinned. "Carol looked very nervous when she had me sign the docket for the trip."

"I couldn't give a fuck about the money, and she did the right thing in booking the plane, so I'll sort that with her."

"I figured you wouldn't miss the money."

"I couldn't give a fuck if it was the last pound in my bank account, you're here, that's all that matters."

We sat down and I beckoned the waitress over. She had been watching our interaction with interest. "Whiskey and a cosmopolitan, please." I said.

"Just a cola please," Alice said. "I had nearly a bottle of champagne of the plane and I have shit loads of work, so I need to think clearly."

"How is work?"

She grinned. "I won the bid from the meeting that I walked out of. Apparently, they liked me feisty and felt my work would suit their brand. Of course, now they want blood for their money and Saffron is freaking out because I'm here and not there. She's going to give herself a migraine!"

"Do you need to go home?"

"Probably," she admitted, "but I'm not going. I can work from here and be here as long as needed. I had the invite for Xander's wedding!"

"Oh?"

"Yeah, he was really upset because he said it looked like something out of a nineteen-eighties American soap, and actually, he

110

was right, not that I told him that, of course. He'd have had a full melt down if I had, but there is a colour code and I have to choose a dress to match, and if the invite is anything to go by, I don't have much hope!"

I laughed. "You'd look good in anything." I cocked my head to one side, "and especially good in absolutely nothing."

Alice blushed. It was the best colour on her, the soft pink that heated her cheeks when I complemented or teased her. Suddenly the world took on the same rosy glow as her face and for just a moment I could forget everything.

"I love you, Alice." I whispered into her ear. "Thank you for being my guardian angel."

She said nothing but the kiss she placed onto my lips said it all.

ALICE

"So, what do we know so far?" I asked Lucien when we'd finally gotten out of bed. Lucien had been insatiable, switching between loving and dominant in a blink of an eye. My body felt tired, the strikes to the skin of my arse cheeks were stinging but, as always, I loved it. I stretched and felt the pull on the flesh of my breasts. My nipples were tender, having been nipped, sucked and flicked by Lucien during our lengthy session. He needed it, needed my total submission and I had given it to him.

I felt safe with Lucien, safe and protected while I put myself under his control. His dominance in the bedroom hit me between the legs every time, my pussy ached for him, swelling and softening to accept his huge length. I'd never been as wet for another man as I was for him, the silken trails onto the creamy skin of my thighs, showed him just how turned on I was. I could never hold back. Even when his commands were to hold the orgasm, it was too much and I always gave in. At those times, the spanks of disapproval just left me wanting more and more.

My body had been made for his.

I winced as I got out of bed, my legs feeling bandy after the hours spent being fucked, and Lucien grinned.

"I love seeing you all spent, knowing it was because of me."

"Don't change the subject." I said walking gingerly to the bathroom. I wrapped a dressing gown around me and crossed to where Lucien was sitting in the window. "Tell me everything you know."

Lucien sighed and rubbed his eyes. I sat down and listened to everything John had told him, a million questions flooding my mind as he spoke. There was more to this story than what he was telling me, I could feel it in my bones. Why would a respected surgeon, one of the leading specialists in his field, change his name? Was it on record? It seemed very extreme to me and something wasn't adding up.

"What are you thinking about?" Lucien asked. "You have a faraway look on your face. Is this all too much for you? Do you want to go home?"

"No." I shook my head vigorously. "Nothing like that. It's just…I have a feeling, Lucien, something isn't right in this story and it's bugging me."

"In what way?"

"You said Jean-Claude was married? Where did his wife go?"

"What do you mean?"

"Did she come to Switzerland after the accident? If so, is she here? If she was your best friend's wife, would she not know more about all this? Have you looked for her?"

Lucien shook his head slowly. "No. I've not a clue where she is, it's taken ten years to find Jean-Claude so finding her may not be so easy."

"But if you've not looked for her then how do you know? You spent the last decade looking for Isabelle, and all the while she was with Jean-Claude who changed his name. Doesn't that make the hairs on your neck prick up just a little?"

Lucien's brow furrowed and he unconsciously began running his finger down the scar that marred his face. "This has been burning like crazy," he told me. "Did you ever play that game when you were a kid, hot and cold, or whatever it was called? It's like that. In London mostly it's cold, but since John sent me the photo of Jean-Claude it's been burning."

I knew the game he was talking about as I'd played it a lot with my older sister, Lucy, mainly when I had hidden something of hers and it gave me a short reprieve before she hit me or told my parents.

"You must be closer than you realise."

He nodded. "It hurts all the time now. Sometimes it's so painful I want to rip my head off! It's strange, usually it's cold." Lucien sighed and stood up. "I'm so tired of having this huge part of me missing, Alice. Yet, I'm so hesitant to believe that it will all be ok. Hettie is in this city somewhere, I'm sure of it, but I have no idea if I will ever see her. She could be so poisoned against me that…" He tailed off and the pain on his face hit me hard.

"It will be ok, Lucien," I said softly. "I really believe that."

"Sometimes I think it will be and then I remember that I was responsible for Ottie and I wonder how it can ever be ok again.

Nothing will bring her back and maybe by trying to find Hettie, I'll be doing more harm than good."

I wrapped my arms around his strong body. "You're her father and you love her. That's more important than anything. It will be ok, Lucien. I promise it will be."

"Fuck, I hope so, Alice. I really, really hope so."

***

I couldn't stop thinking about Jean-Claude's wife Clarisse, Isabelle's best friend. I went around and around in circles trying to piece it all together but none of it added up to a sensible answer. What wasn't I seeing? While Lucien fielded work calls in the hotel room, I took myself off to the lounge to work. Or try to work, at least. Clarisse was the missing piece I was so sure of it. I was no private investigator and had no idea what I was going to do to find out if I was right, but something was bugging me, and I had to know what.

I tapped away on my laptop replying to emails, ignoring Saffron's increasingly irate messages that were filling up my mobile voicemail. I had so much work to do that I visualised myself drowning in quicksand. Shit, I was going to drop all the balls I was just about keeping in the air, if I wasn't careful. The new client was already demanding my soul and when I finished the emails, I started reading the brief. Saffron had been on about me hiring another assistant, mainly because she wanted to be able to boss someone else around, but I was beginning to think she was right.

The brief was confusing and not anything like I'd bid for. They'd changed everything. Absolutely everything. With a sigh I began making notes in my book of ideas and concepts, each one being replaced by the next amendment I encountered. In the end I gave them a call and they agreed to send a version of the brief they actually wanted.

I sent Saffron an email with several tasks on it and then, putting my feet up on the chair in front of me and balancing my laptop on my knee, I opened a browser and began to search. Jean-Claude's history with his previous surname was missing from every medical website I could find. It was as though he hadn't ever existed. Slowly I typed in his new name. Page after page came up on the search engine, about his skills as a surgeon, about his volunteering at the Zurich psychiatric rehab facility and everything possible about his interests. Nothing about a wife, nothing about Isabelle, nothing that would have made him real.

He was a surgeon. The top surgeon in Switzerland, as it happened, so why would he volunteer at a facility for people with complex mental health issues. I clicked on a few more websites. Nothing in his background that would suggest he'd had any experience in psychiatric medicine. Was his background even real?

It seemed to be an incredibly complicated way to hide from a friend whose wife and family you'd stolen, but then, the whole situation was incredibly complex. Jean-Claude was a dead end. So where was his wife?

I picked up my mobile phone and dialled the office. "Carol?" I said, when Lucien's PA answered the private line. "Can you get me John Frank's phone number, but don't let on to Lucien that I've asked."

Carol sounded really uncomfortable as she put me on hold to find the number. When she came back on the line she was hesitant.

"It's ok, Carol, really, I'm not doing anything sinister, I'm just looking into something and I don't want to get Lucien's hopes up."

Carol sounded disgruntled and muttered a few things under her breath that sounded like, 'I shouldn't be doing this', but gave me the number and hung up without saying goodbye. I understood why, she probably thought my intentions were as crazy as when I demanded an immediate flight to Zurich, and she knew very little so that was probably driving her mad. Carol usually knew everything. Lucien needed her to because his work life was so manic someone had to control it and she was exactly the right person for that thankless task.

I looked at the number and glanced back at my laptop. I had an idea but I wasn't a PI and the last thing I wanted to do was fuck this up. I took a deep breath, closed my search history and dialled John Frank.

LUCIEN

I was bored shitless. Alice had gone out. Apparently, she needed new clothes and same-day delivery wasn't as convenient as actually buying them from a shop. Which made me suspicious because Alice hated clothes shopping.

John had told me to lay low and I got the feeling that he wished I'd not made the trip. There was very little I could do, bar pacing the hotel room like a mad zoo animal, and the mountain of work I had to get through didn't inspire me. I could think of nothing but beating Jean-Claude to a bloody pulp. The cunt. I was driving myself crazy questioning the validity of our friendship, an affair with Isabelle, the way he wormed himself into Hettie's affections that I wanted to kill him.

Fuck, I was losing myself.

Again.

I looked down at my watch. Alice had been gone ages and my phone had stayed silent. Usually she texted me when she was shopping, sending lots of photos, some guaranteed to have me waiting for her with a raging erection. Today, she had been completely off-grid and it really bothered me.

It felt as though she was up to something.

Which bothered me even more.

I trusted Alice more than I'd trusted anyone, bar John, since Ottie died, but I couldn't shift the feeling that something was going on. I didn't think for one moment that she'd cheat on me, and in any case, who did she know in Zurich, but there was something bugging me, and I had to resist the temptation to use my usual methods to track her down.

I threw my phone down on the sofa and tried to focus on work. Decisions had to be made, decisions I really needed to be in London for, but leaving wasn't an option. Fucked economy or not, I would rather have lost the business than take the risk on my family.

Family.

I didn't have a family. I had a wife, a living child and a child lying in a lonely grave because I put her there, and I had Alice. She was my world, but sometimes, an agreement was simpler. I shouldn't have dragged her into this.

I desperately wanted a drink. I needed to get obliterated because the stress was driving me crazy but I didn't opt for a whisky because I knew I wouldn't stop at one. Instead, I went to the gym. There I had control. It gave me head space, it eased the stress and when I was punching the boxing bag, the bag had Jean-Claude's face on it. It made me feel better.

Much better.

***

Alice was back in the room when I made my way, aching and wincing, back up from the gym. I'd pushed it as hard as I could then went further, anything to blot out the extreme anxiety that was crippling my brain. Physical demands on my body took the voices away and while I was concentrating on one rep at a time, I couldn't hear the screams in the dark, the last gasping breaths and the sounds of my heart shattering.

"Hi!" She said, from where she was sat on the bed, surrounded by bags. Lots and lots of bags. If I thought her silence was strange, the number of bags made everything far more questionable. Alice hated shopping. She bought one or two items when she had to, otherwise she spent her days in casual clothes, or, my preferred choice, naked.

"Hey." I said, flopping down in the chair and opening a bottle of water. "Good day?"

Alice shrugged. "You know me, shopping isn't my most favourite thing to do." She stood up and a couple of the bags fell from the bed. Alice stepped over them and walked to me. "My most favourite thing to do, is you…" She said huskily. "Over and over, but you know that, don't you?" Alice leaned over me, her hair falling over my face. "I've been thinking about you all day." I wrapped my hands in her hair, pulling it back from her face. Her eyes were shining, and she had a look of elation on her face.

"Alice? Has something happened today?"

She paused and took my hands from her hair as she stood up. She seemed to be in another place, somewhere that I couldn't reach.

"Alice?"

"I need you to trust me," she said softly. "Please trust me and don't ask me anything, not yet. I'd have to lie to you and that would be the worst thing."

"You weren't just shopping today, were you?"

"No." Alice shook her head. "I did shop but… please, Lucien, I need to be sure about something, before I tell you. Not because I want to keep something from you, but because I absolutely have to be right."

"Ok." I said, although I couldn't keep the unhappiness out of my voice. Alice looked worried and bit down on her lip but said nothing. It felt strange to have something there between us and even stranger that she was keeping something from me. I know she would have her reasons but there were too many secrets and too many unknowns, that another one just made me feel more shit.

"Ok?"

"It's fine, Alice."

"It doesn't feel fine."

I stood up and walked towards the bathroom. "You have your reasons, let's leave it at that. I'm going for a shower."

Alice said nothing more. She sat down in the window seat and picked her laptop off the floor where it had been discarded. "I'll get some work done, then."

"Good plan."

There was worry and concern on Alice's face that she tried to disguise with a smile. I realised why she was keeping something from me, and why it was so important.

It was to do with the reason why we were in Zurich.

She had to be sure.

I understood.

Hettie and Ottie.

ALICE

Lucien looked downcast when he walked into the bathroom. The trouble was, I had nothing to tell him that would make sense and I was sure he would ask me to stop what I was doing. I was also sure he'd feel like I'd gone behind his back, and I supposed I had.

I waited for him to turn the shower on before I opened my web browser. Meeting John Frank had been an eye-opener. I'd told him my theory on Clarisse, Jean-Claude's wife and he'd had the same thoughts as me – she was the missing piece of the puzzle. There was a risk, of course, that Isabelle would recognise me if I was not careful, and run off again, taking Hettie with her, assuming that Hettie was in Zurich. John hadn't seen her, but Jean-Claude was seriously wealthy, so she was likely to be in one of the most exclusive schools. I'd wondered if she had been placed in a boarding school, but John had not managed to track her down anywhere. He'd told me how he'd looked back over previous angles using Jean-Claude's new name, but nothing had come up.

Where were they hiding Hettie?

John's team were covering all angles, and he'd made it very clear I wasn't to get in the way. It had not been my intention, but I was personally invested in Lucien's happiness and I would take on the devil himself to get some answers.

There was a link somewhere. I just wasn't seeing it, but, every time Clarisse popped into my head, my stomach fluttered. Had they hidden her too?

I stared blankly at google then opened one of my design tools, I usually used it to brainstorm ideas when I was with a client. It turned thoughts and ideas into a spider graph and was useful for putting a design plan together. That day, however, I used to it to create at 'what I knew' graph and, in reverse, 'what I didn't know'

By the time I'd finished there was four gaping holes – what name Isabelle was using, what name Hettie was using, the missing wife and the final piece, why was Jean-Claude volunteering at a rehab facility for mental illness when he had no qualifications in that field.

Jean-Claude – Isabelle – Hettie – Clarisse – Facility – Names - Jean-Claude – Isabelle – Hettie – Clarisse – Facility – Names - Jean-

Claude – Isabelle – Hettie – Clarisse – Facility – Names - Jean-Claude – Isabelle – Hettie – Clarisse – Facility – Names – round and round and round until I had steam coming out of my ears but the answer was piercingly loud.

I knew where Clarisse was.

Fuck.

What now?

***

"You're very quiet." Lucien said over dinner. He'd looked pale since he had gotten out of the shower and kept absentmindedly running his finger down his scar. It was normally a silver colour, with a tinge of pink, but since we'd been in Zurich it looked an angry red, the colour desperately at odds with his pallor.

"Sorry, Lucien. I'm just thinking…" I took a deep breath in.

"About?"

I looked at him. There was a hope in his eyes I'd not seen since I'd been here, but he looked tired, weary almost, as though being so close was taking a huge toll on his energy levels. Lucien was the most energetic person I'd ever met, and his insatiable sexual prowess was never dampened by hours in the gym or hours at work but these past couple of weeks had taken so much from him. I wanted to tell him my theory, desperately, but I knew how fearful he was that the opportunity in Zurich would be missed or ruined irreparably, that I kept quiet. This was my task. I just had to figure out how to prove I was right.

I turned my gaze down to my food and Lucien shifted backwards in his chair.

"Alice? What are you thinking about?"

I chewed on my lip. Lucien watched me as I rested my forehead on my hand, arm bent at the elbow. "I have a theory." I said quietly. "I feel certain I am right, but it will take a lot to prove it."

"Will you tell me your theory?" I shook my head slowly. "Why?"

"What if I'm wrong, Lucien? What if I tell you and you get more hopeful and I'm completely wrong?"

"I'll live with it." He said moving forward to brush a fallen strand of hair from my head.

"Will you give me a couple of days to see if I'm right? If it's a dead end, then I'll tell you?"

"And if it's not?"

"Then I'll tell you." I held his palm to my cheek. His hand was warm and soft against my face. "Whatever happens, I'll tell you."

"Ok." Lucien said quietly, rubbing his thumb against my jaw line. "Ok, Alice, I'll trust you. I trust you with everything else, why should this be any different."

"I love you." I whispered, moving his palm to my lips and kissing it.

"I love you too, beautiful Alice." Lucien took his hand back and placed his knife and fork on his plate, the food mostly untouched. "What say we go upstairs, and I'll show you how much."

I looked down at my own plate of barely touched food. "I say, yes please."

LUCIEN

Alice's body glistened beneath me. Her high, swollen breasts were cupped in her hands and she had a look of bliss on her face. Her mouth had fallen open and barely audible sighs were escaping from the moist lips. Fuck she was gorgeous, and sexy and completely perfect for me. I lazily ran my tongue over the hard nub between her legs, and she moved her hips up towards me. She always tasted delicious, womanly and sweet, but more so this evening, her body was calling to me and I responded in the only way I knew how.

I slid my fingers into her warm channel, feeling the tight muscles clench around them. Her eyes rolled back, and she sighed, a smile curving her lips. "Fuck my fingers." I whispered, my mouth back on her clitoris. "Show me how you like it."

Alice began to rock against my fingers, moving her hips back and forth. She was silky wet and the sweet spot I was rolling my tongue over swelled further. I loved how responsive she was, how open her body was to me and how she matched my insatiability. We were the same – demanding, controlling and dominant – but in such different ways. Alice had no idea how much control she had over me, that she could make me putty in her hands with a look or a suggestion. She also had no idea that the most beautiful I found her to be was when she had just got up, her hair sticking up at all angles, wearing my tee-shirt, unable to talk until she'd had coffee.

I began to kiss the soft skin of her thighs, using my thumb to stroke her clitoris. Alice's sighed turned to gasps as she moved faster against my fingers. "That's it, dirty girl," I murmured, nipping the porcelain skin, "show me." I watched her pull at her breasts, pinching the rosy nipples as she arched her back, the tell-tale flush of desire on her cheeks. The muscles of her pussy were gripping harder and her breath was coming in pants. "Not yet," I said huskily, "not without me."

I pulled my fingers from her. My cock, painfully hard, was already shiny with beads of pre-cum and I knew I wouldn't last long, but from the groans coming from Alice as she teased and flicked her nipples, she wouldn't last much longer either.

"You want me?"

"Always." She moaned. I leaned over her and took one of her nipples in my mouth, cupping my hand around the heavy breast. She had sensational tits, full and high on her rib cage and so sensitive that I could make her cum just by playing with them. "Lucien, please…"

"Please what?"

"Please fuck me, I need you to. I'm so close, Lucien, please…"

The soft begs made my cock twitch. With a final tug on her nipple with my teeth, I guided my cock into her, slamming in as deeply as I could.

"Ah," she cried out, the rapture in her voice ringing out. "Yes."

Alice wrapped her legs around me, and we moved together. Her body was so soft and voluptuous, the curves of her body excited me more than any other body ever had. The fizzing in my cock became bubbles that seemed to pop against my skin until Alice tensed and her hot channel gripped my pulsating cock so tightly, I saw stars.

"I'm coming." She cried, "fuck, Lucien, I'm coming."

As Alice gave into her orgasm, I let go, filling her with the juice of my pleasure, wrapping my hands in her hair and pushing into her until every drop had spilled.

"Oh my God," she whispered against my cheek. "Oh my God."

I turned my head and kissed her mouth. "I fucking love you."

Alice smiled. "I fucking love you too."

***

I could hear hushed talking as I roused. I had no idea of the time, nor when I'd fallen asleep. I'd slept well, having Alice's body wrapped around me always helped me sleep well, she kept the demons away. I stretched and strained to hear. Alice was on the phone in the lounge area, whispering as loudly as she could. She hadn't noticed I'd woken but kept stealing worried glanced over to the bed. I knew it was the *thing* she was keeping from me, the hairs on the back of my neck were upright and prickling against the pillow.

What did she know?

I trusted her implicitly but it did bother me, more than I cared to admit, that she knew something about my family that I didn't. I hated all of this. Hated that Hettie was in the same town as me yet she still may have been on the moon. I hated that I couldn't confront Jean-Claude for breaking every single brotherhood code since the dawn of time. I longed to punch his fucking face to a pulp and leave the demons to take his soul, like they took mine.

"Really? And you're sure?" Alice said down the phone, turning her back to me and cupping her hand around the microphone. "You're absolutely sure you can get me in?"

She listened intently and then said, "thank you. I'll be there." Alice looked down at the clock on the table. "Thirty minutes. Fine, see you then."

She glanced back over to the bed and then, putting her phone on the table, crossed the room towards the bathroom.

A thousand questions flooded my mine and the familiar excruciating anxiety twisted my stomach. What if she fucked it all up? Could we ever get past that? Losing Alice would be unthinkable, but to lose Hettie when I was so close – I'd not get over that so easily and if it was because of Alice, it could break us.

Probably for always.

Fuck, Alice, what are you up to?

Then the demon whispered, and I stopped listening to Alice.

You're a bad man, you killed your daughter. You deserve what you get. You deserve to lose Alice. You deserve to never see Hettie again. You deserve everything you get, Lucien Ross.

You are a bad man.

A bad, bad man.

You killed Ottie.

It was all your fault.

You don't deserve Alice.

She will leave you.

You break everything.

Lucien Ross is bad.

I got out of bed and walked across the room to the bathroom. Alice was in the shower, I could hear her muffled singing and the running of water. Screwing up my eyes tightly and rubbing my temples with the tips of my fingers, I tried to block out the voices. I wanted so desperately to send them away, but they were telling me the truth. I did break everything. I didn't deserve Alice and the most painful, heart-breaking one of all, I killed Ottie. There was no getting away from that, despite what Alice believed. Her faith in me would prove misguided and I would lose her. It would happen. But, at that moment I needed her warmth and comfort more than I needed the air I breathed. She had come for me. She was here for me. She left a brand new client for me. Until the day she walked away, she would always be my guardian angel. She would always be my love.

I didn't deserve her, but I was fucking glad I got her.

Alice.

Angel.

I reached for the handle and opened the door.

ALICE

Lucien opened the door and there was something in his face that stopped me singing, the words sticking in my throat. He was grey, the scar on his face a vivid, angry red and his hands, clenched into fists were shaking.

"Lucien?" I asked stepping to the opening of the walk-in shower, "are you alright?"

He shook his head slowly. I'd seen him like this only a couple of times before and I knew the demons in his head were gripping tightly. I could almost see them beside him, the ghosts of his past whispering vitriol into his ears, telling him that all the bad stuff he held onto was true. Looking at him literally falling apart in front of me, made me even more determined to do what I could to help resolve it.

I walked towards him, unsure if he could see me. Lucien was always so strong, so controlled, so demanding that it was all the more unbearable to see him crumpling. The first time I'd seen him collapse under the weight of his guilt was the day he'd nearly died. His whole body had begun to shake, and I wrapped my wet self around him, holding him tightly, willing my body to be strong enough to keep him upright. His muscles, so defined, were digging into me painfully, but I shut my mind to it and held on. Eventually, as the goosebumps began to spread over my skin and my own body began to shiver because of the chill, his shaking slowed, and I could feel his heart rate return to a normal beat.

"You're cold." He whispered, burying his head in my neck.

"It doesn't matter." I whispered back, kissing the top of his head.

"Fuck, Alice, I felt like I was dying." He said, pulling his face from my neck and wrapping his hands in my wet hair. "There was a pain in my heart, I thought I was going to have a heart attack. Shit."

I placed my hand over his chest and felt the regular pulse. "Lucien, go home. Go back to London. I'll stay here with John but take a break before you send yourself crazy."

"I can't."

"But you can't do anything here, you can't even go out, it's no wonder you're feeling anxious, you're trapped like a caged lion. Go back to London and focus on work, leave the team and me here, I have a lead, John's team are all here now, they are making progress…"

Lucien didn't hear me. "The mighty Lucien Ross isn't so mighty, is he? What a let-down, hey Alice? When you could have a hero instead."

"A hero? What are you talking about?" I was feeling really cold, my skin had a tinge of blue and I was shivering. Lucien didn't seem to notice because he was lost in his own revulsion. "Lucien?"

"Oh, come on Alice," he snapped. "Don't forget I saw you with him."

Realisation dawned on me. "Oh, for fuck's sake, Lucien, not this again? There is nothing between Zac and me, apart from being in the same place at the same time. Don't try and make me feel shit just because you do."

Lucien nodded sadly. "I do feel shit, Alice. I feel so shit that I want to fucking scream. My daughter is here, somewhere, with the man who was supposed to be my best friend, who also has my wife. The same wife who wants my daughter to be adopted. Shit doesn't even come close to how I feel. I'm so fucking angry that I'm being eaten alive by hate. I didn't think I could feel so much hatred but if Jean-Claude crossed my path, I honestly think I'd kill him."

"Because of Hettie?"

"Because of it all," he admitted. "Because he took my life away."

"I guess that will include Isabelle." I don't know why I said it. I would always be scared of the hold Isabelle had over Lucien, because even though he denied any feelings towards her, other than explosive anger, she was the mother of his children and the first love of his life. That was a hard thing for me to forget.

Lucien looked at me and sighed. "I'm allowed to be angry that she walked out on me when I was so ill," he said. "It doesn't mean that I want her back, Alice, it means I'm really fucking angry, that's all. The more I think about things, the more I find out, the more I realise that she probably had an affair with Jean-Claude, even though Clarisse was her best friend. Betrayal is hard to swallow, even ten years on."

"Is that why you got so angry about Zac?"

127

"Probably, although him being a superhero doesn't fucking help matters, Alice." Lucien pulled me closer and kissed my mouth. "I'm jealous of anyone you speak to, you're so fucking sexy I expect them to whisk you away to a life of normalcy, not keep you tied to a life full of my shit."

"Imagine how boring that would be." I said softly, walking us back into the shower, the warmth from the water beginning to thaw out my skin. "Imagine not being able to drag Mr Normal and Boring into the shower…" I stroked my hands down the strong muscles of his chest, drawing under them with my fingertips, "because he isn't sexy, he's dull, imagine not being able to kneel down before him and take his glorious cock into my mouth, because normal and boring don't have glorious cocks." I knelt beneath the shower, the water raining down above me. Lucien's cock was twitching under his boxer shorts as I slowly lowered his underwear, freeing the hardening member. "Imagine not being able to run my tongue along his cock, knowing it would turn him on to feel my mouth wrapped around him, sucking hard."

"Imagine." Lucien sighed blissfully as I took his erection into my mouth. His hands went to my hair as I pleasured his cock, teasing and stroking with my tongue, along the velvet skin that encased the hardness. Everything about Lucien turned me on, his face, his muscular body, his strength of character, his faults and fears and his beautiful, sensational cock from which I got so much gratification. I could feel the fizzing of pre-cum under his skin and knowing I turned him on just as much as he did for me, went straight to my pussy, swelling the lips and inflaming the nub at my centre. I kept my mouth around him as I used my fingers to slowly stroke myself, the silken juice flowing as the pleasure increased. I took Lucien's cock deeply into my mouth and his hands tightened on my head. Lucien pushed in and out of my mouth, holding my head still as he gave me his length. My fingers fucked my pussy while Lucien fucked my mouth. My cries of pleasure were muffled but caused him to groan as the vibrations added to the sensations of my mouth around his cock.

"Alice! Fuck! Yes! Alice."

He was close, I could feel it in the urgency of his thrusting, and I could feel my own body responding to him and my fingers, buried deep in me.

"I have to be in you, Alice." Lucien moaned. "Now, I have to be in you."

In one swift movement, Lucien had me flat, on my front, on the floor of the shower, his body on top of mine. The ceramic was hard against my nipples, erect like bullets, and the weight of his body, pushed my hips into the floor. Lava flowed through me as Lucien spread my legs and guided his cock into me, the hardness stretching the tight muscles of my pussy.

"Ah." I cried out as he slammed into me over and over until I saw stars. I longed to move, to touch him, to stroke his body and feel his lips on mine, but I was immobile by the pressure of him on my back. He had taken control back, he'd needed it and I willingly gave myself to him and let him fuck me until his body jerked and his groans filled the shower with sound. A few seconds later the fire in me exploded and I came loudly, my body tensing, the muscles in my pussy clenched around his cock as the orgasm ripped through me and I lowered my face to the floor, spent.

"You are so fucking sexy, Alice." Lucien murmured into my ear, nipping my lobe with his teeth. "So, fucking sexy. But remember, you're mine, only mine. No one else can have you."

"Always." I whispered back, reaching behind me to take hold of his hands. "Always."

Lucien shifted enough for me to move out from under him. My hips and nipples felt bruised from the shower tray, but my body was enjoying the post-fuck glow.

He wrapped me in his arms, and we lay under the raining water, silently.

"I love you, Alice." Lucien said eventually. "There isn't anyone else for me, just you. Tell me you want me, not the hero in khaki."

"I want you." I said, kissing his shoulder. "Only you. You're it for me, Lucien. There couldn't be anyone for me, it was only you from the moment I walked into your office. You're my life, demons and all."

"When all this shit is over, Alice Addison, I'm going to marry you."

"You are?" I squeaked.

"You'd better fucking believe it."

Then he kissed me, and it was a kiss like no other before. It was the kiss that promised happily ever after.

LUCIEN

I went back to London. It went against every instinct I had but Alice was right, I was trapped in a hotel room, pacing up and down like a zoo animal, unable to do anything in the search for Hettie. Zurich was so small, if I went out, chances were that I'd bump into Jean-Claude or Isabelle and fuck everything up completely. That I didn't know what Alice was up to, also left a bad taste in my mouth.

She left before I did to go on her mystery mission. She gave me an absent-minded kiss, her thoughts clearly elsewhere and told me that she loved me, but she had left the room so quickly, I barely saw her go. I could have tracked her, I had ways of finding Alice, but I didn't want to know. It was easier to deal with the anxiety of the situation than it was to really know what she had planned. Alice was doing it for me. She had no other reason to keep anything from me, apart from to protect me, as I would protect her.

The car dropped me at the office. There was no point going home, it was too quiet and empty, and I would have only paced in my self-created prison, so I went to work. I'd neglected it for too long and the contracts we'd fought so hard to win, were looking shaky. If I didn't give it my full attention, the get-out-clauses would be used and that would be extremely bad for business. It was rocky enough as it was, without deliberately screwing things for Ross Industries.

We'd ride whatever storm the political uncertainty brought to us, but I couldn't keep focusing on my personal life without giving direction to my staff. They were a talented bunch, hard working and committed, but their interest would wane without me firing on all cylinders and that would be disastrous.

I nodded at the receptionist as I crossed the foyer to the lift. I had no interest in making small talk with anyone, so I pushed the button for my office and kept the main floor for another time. Carol was on the phone when I arrived, so I gave her a small wave and walked into my office. There were piles of documents waiting for me to read, all important to the bid we'd won, that I felt my heart sink. I wasn't sure I wanted this life anymore, the stress and endless demands for my attention. I'd worked so hard to build up the business, sacrificing everything to make it a success but I wondered if I'd not worked so hard, not tried so hard, not wanted to give Isabelle everything she craved, that maybe my marriage would have lasted.

Perhaps we would have been happier living a less materialistic life and maybe our lives would have been richer if we'd not fought against being products of our pasts. Maybe I should have dealt with my feelings towards my fucktard alcoholic father, instead of trying to prove I was nothing like him.

I remember the days of being hungry while he snored drunkenly on the sofa, my mum trying to make a meal from whatever money she'd managed to hide from him. It was a shit, fucked up life and I hated him. I hated him for breaking us, for taking the light from my Mum's eyes and for being a disgusting, piss-soaked slob who occasionally lashed out with a fist or a belt. I vowed I would never be like him, never be that kind of selfish cunt who took everything from his family, but I had. I was absolutely a product of my past.

For years I drank infrequently, then the demons got louder, and time after time, the whiskey blotted the voices out. I'd become too much like him in the bleak decade that followed Ottoline's death that the self-revulsion ate away at me. Then Alice came along and she brought me back into the world, back to life and gave me hope that I could be a better man.

I dialled her number. I listened to the ringing tone before the voicemail clicked in. "Hey you, it's me. I'm in the office. I'll be here most of the evening, call me when you're finished. Love you."

Fuck, what was she up to?

I pulled the first document to me and began to read, forcing my thoughts to focus on the task, not on Alice's whereabouts. Had I made a huge mistake coming back?

"Lucien! You're back!" Lana said, walking into my office, not bothering to knock as usual. "Thank fuck. I'm not going to try and tell you how to run your business but seriously, you disappearing all the time, is making everyone nervous, unless you're Superman off to save the day." She narrowed her eyes. "Maybe Superman after a battle with a shit load of kryptonite. Where have you been?"

I ignored her question. "Are you suggesting I look like shit, Lana?"

132

She grinned. "Well you've never done it for me Lucien, but honestly, you look like you need a month of sleep. Work or personal?"

"Personal."

"Then say no more, but three staff have resigned this week, and I need you to sign this so I can replace them. Carol is quite the stickler for the rules."

I took the form from her. "Who's resigned?"

"A couple of marketing assistants, it's ok, there are plenty of candidates to replace them, and one from the design department."

"Alice can have the work." I said quickly. "For now, at least. I don't want to rush a new designer, the contracts we're working on are quite specific, lots of US government security hoops to jump through, that will take time."

"And where is Alice?"

"She's away."

"I know! Saffron is tearing out her hair. The phones are ringing off the hook and Alice is barely answering an email. Saffron may be the first victim of Alice's success."

"Do we have anyone low down the pecking order who can help her?"

"There is the new girl in the post room, but don't we need her?"

"Is she any good?"

"She seems ok…"

"Send her up to help Saffron and send someone from the admin team down to the post room."

"They'll not like that!"

"Tough."

"Lucien, are we really paying a staff member to support your girlfriend's company, when she should be here to do it herself?"

"She is doing something for me, Lana." I said crossly. "And while she is, we'll help her."

"Alright." Lana said, clearly jolted. I knew she was watching the news just as closely as I was and was trying, in her own way, to remind me that there was no room for overspending or being blasé with the accounts. She meant well, Lana had worked for me for years and she was my most trusted employee, able to stand up to me when none of the others could. Until Alice joined the team, anyway. "No offence meant, it's just…"

"I know. It's shit out there."

"Will we be alright?

"If the country really is fucked, we'll be ok for a year or two. After that, who knows. I'll do whatever I can to make sure we keep afloat."

"Maybe take fewer private jets, Lucien." Lana said, raising her eyebrow. "Fly economy next time."

"Not that it is any of your business, Lana, but it wasn't something that could wait for an economy flight out of London. Is there anything else?"

"Nope, just your signature." Lana nodded at the documents in my hands. I signed and she took them from me. "You know, Lucien. You don't look well. Perhaps see a doctor."

"It's just stress Lana."

"Since when did you suffer from stress."

"You wouldn't believe me if I told you."

"And there I was thinking Alice was good for you."

"She is, Lana."

Lana raised an eyebrow. "So why have you looked like shit since you met her?"

"Coincidence, and besides, you're hardly going to tell me I look hot, are you!"

Lana grinned and crossed my office to the door. "No, I'm not, but Alice on the other hand…"

"Don't even fucking joke!"

I heard her laughing all the way to the lift.

ALICE

"You're sure this will get me in?" I asked looking down at the security pass John had given me. Excruciating nerves kicked in and I wanted to be violently sick. What if I fucked up and blew this whole thing for Lucien? How would he ever forgive me if I lost him his daughter? Isabelle had seen me once, would she remember me? Shit, shit, shit. What was I doing?

"Absolutely sure. You have access to every floor in the place, Alice. Money talks, it buys people and silence."

"I'm not sure it could buy me." I muttered, swallowing down a suffocating ball of acid that was burning my throat.

"No? Then you may be one of the only ones. Everyone has a price Alice."

"How much did this person," I waggled the security pass, "sell their soul for?"

"No mortgage and private schools for his kids."

"Fuck."

"Indeed." John grinned. "This is your job, Alice. You made the connection so you have to see it through. We have other leads to follow. We have to find Hettie before they realise they're being followed. Isabelle has seen me a couple of times, I have someone else tailing her now."

"And Hettie?"

"Still no sign of her. We know where they live so we have someone on permanent surveillance of the house."

"How do they not know?"

"Because we are shit-hot at our job, Alice." John said without a hint of conceit.

"Have you always done this?" I asked him, running my fingertip over the barcode.

"I was in special forces for years, encountered a bomb and lost the lower half of my leg. My training has come in handy for hours sat watching people."

"Oh." I didn't know what to say, but it seemed more and more that everyone carried scars from something through their life. "I'm not sure I can do this."

135

"Alice, it's a research pass, not entry into MI5. You just have to take your time and find out what you can. If anyone asks, I have papers for you showing that you are doing a PhD in psychiatric medicine and this is part of your study programme."

"I'm doing what?" I asked aghast. "I don't know the first thing about psychiatry."

"You don't need to because we've done the work for you. Everything is in here. Read it over and over until you're word perfect. Your university accreditation is in there, with a letter from your tutor."

"How?" My head was spinning, and I was wishing I'd left well alone. "How do I have a tutor?"

"I told you Alice, everyone has a price."

"Does Lucien know about these costs?" I wondered how he kept it all from his sharp-eyed accountant and even sharper-eyed PA.

"Lucien knows all of it. Lucien would spend his last penny to find Hettie. I've been working for him for years…"

"I know. He trusts you."

"And so he should," John replied gruffly. "I've never let him down on anything and I'm not going to start now. It's been a long process to get to this point, it took us years to find Ottie's grave, Isabelle left no trace at all. It was only by chance that we got to Zurich and found out Jean-Claude had changed his name. There is no record of the old him anywhere and we still can't find out what name Isabelle and Hettie are using. I am not leaving Zurich until this case is cracked, though Alice, Lucien knows that. He also knows we wouldn't spend money unless we had to."

"I know." I nodded slowly and took a deep breath in. "It's just, so much money."

"It's nothing when you need to complete the puzzle."

"I suppose."

John smiled at me. "Lucien needed someone like you, a badass. You're good for him Alice." It sounded strange to have such a compliment from someone like John, but I took it with a grin.

"Thanks John. Although if I screw this up, you'll be thinking very differently!"

"You won't fuck it up, Alice. You're as invested in this as we are."

"Maybe more so."

"Maybe. Now get going. Read the pack and be ready for tomorrow. Get a bus, you're a poor PhD student, remember. There is a timetable in there and directions to the hospital."

"Hospital? I thought it was an exclusive mental health rehab facility."

"Call it what you will, at the end of the day the poor bastards in there are pumped full of drugs while they have their heads messed with."

I finished the coffee in front of me. It was stone cold and too sweet, but it gave me a moment of respite from the swirling fear in my mind. I was so certain that Jean-Claude's wife held the key to all of this, but the task ahead of me was mind-numbingly terrifying. All I could hear in my frozen mind was my drama teacher's harsh comments *'You are one of the most unbelievable trees I've ever seen, Alice Addison.'* If I couldn't even be a tree, how the fuck was I going to be believable as a graduate of psychiatry?

***

"Hey you, it's me. I'm in the office. I'll be here most of the evening, call me when you're finished. Love you." I listened to Lucien's voicemail over and over, feeling the sting of tears behind my eyes. He had so much faith in me, showing just how much by taking the plane back to London, and I was frightened of blowing that faith from the sky. I mulled over the conversation John and I had, that anyone could be bought for the right price. The documents on the table, the ID card and a whole history that wasn't mine, was proof enough. Shit.

Did I have a price too?

I poured a large vodka from the mini bar and sat with my feet up, papers on my lap, staring out of the window over Zurich. It looked to be such a beautiful city, but it would forever be associated with this moment. Like Paris, Zurich would be off my visit list forever.

I took a long drink and gagged. Neat vodka wasn't the best idea. Tipping the papers from my lap I walked over to the mini bar and added a large bottle of tonic. I may have been feeling stressed but giving myself alcohol poisoning wouldn't make anything better. I sat back down and resignedly picked up the papers. There was so much to learn and so little time to learn it, the pressure was on and it was all of my own making.

Shit.

LUCIEN

I had thrown myself into work, called staff meetings and even did a vomit-inducing work out in the gym but nothing took my mind from wondering where Alice was. She hadn't returned my call, but she hadn't left the hotel all afternoon and the silence from her was excruciating. Why wasn't she calling? I felt completely helpless and the handing over of the control I kept such a tight grip on was alien and unnerving.

Come on, Alice, ring.

In the end I went home, taking piles of paper with me that Carol had been insisting I do something with at all day. She had given me a look that screamed disappointment and her patience was well and truly frayed by the time she left.

I understood her frustration, I wouldn't want to work for me at the moment either and with Alice and John not responding to my calls the day was sending my mood to hell.

The apartment was stuffy and dark when I arrived home. I turned on some music and opened a couple of windows, letting the cool evening air in. My apartment, so minimalist, usually calmed me but there was no calm to be found. Every time my phone rang or beeped I jumped like a scalded cat but it never was the two people I most wanted to speak to.

What the fuck was going on in Zurich?

In the end I accepted an invitation for drinks with an acquaintance I knew from the various City boards I was on and steeled myself for the effort required in being sociable. I knew it probably wouldn't end well, 'no thank you' wasn't the correct response to another drink but equally a fuzzy head in the morning would be the worst way to start another shit day.

Sighing I opened a beer and headed to the shower.

***

It was as predictable as feared. I met ten of my least-irritating acquaintances at a private members club in Soho for the usual back slapping, cigar smoking shit that I used to revel in. Vintage

139

champagne flowed from whichever flashy fuck decided to wave their black credit card at the scantily clad waitress, who looked as though she'd rather gouge out her own eyeballs with a spoon than serve the pompous arses. The notes that got tucked into the waistband of her skirt must have cheered her up, but the smiles were false and the accepting of the innuendos was through gritted teeth.

She was about the same age as Alice.

I felt old.

Old, battered and broken.

She made me miss Alice.

I longed for a fuck, mainly to release the tension that tightened every muscle in my body, but as I watched the waitress move, I craved the feel of Alice's body moving with mine. I looked at the girl and thought how I would have once made a play for her, used her, had an agreement that put me in complete control, and left her when my interest waned. She was sexy, big tits, curved hips and a plump mouth that was painted glossy red, and I knew I would have easily pulled her and fucked her any which way I chose. She knew what she was doing when she accepted the compliments from the men I was with, she got money thrown at her, but I knew it was me who had caught her interest. I could see it in stolen glances and the way she pushed out her tits when she served me. She was exciting in an obvious way, very fuckable and judging by the sly smile she proffered when she served me, she was also really fucking dirty.

It had been awhile since I'd had *really fucking dirty*. I didn't want the desires of my old life creeping into what I had with Alice so kept play within her limits but the stress I was under was making me crave all sorts of shit that I'd left behind. I didn't trust myself. The more champagne I drank, the more I was sharing lingering glances with the waitress. If I wasn't careful, I would fuck my life up completely.

"Does anything else take your fancy, Mr Ross?" She asked me in a breathy voice.

"No." I replied shortly, averting my gaze to focus on a distasteful painting on the wall. I couldn't look at her. She was leaning over me, her shirt unbuttoned to show a creamy cleavage and plump breasts. Then, fuck it, I looked and wished I hadn't. Her nipples were hard under the shirt and without meaning too, I licked my lips.

"Oh look, Lucien is up to his old tricks." Someone slurred.

"Not at all." I replied sharply, sitting up and leaning away from her.

The waitress stood up with a look of disappointment on her face and collected empty glasses before walking away from the table. The scent of her perfume lingered, too harsh to be alluring and not floral enough to be like Alice. She was nothing like Alice.

I wanted to get out of there.

"Come on Lucien, drink up." Basil said, his words thick with the effects of the champagne. "We're going onwards."

"I'm going home." I muttered. Home for a wank and a coffee before I did anything I would regret.

"Fuck going home, man, what's the matter with you. We're going dancing!" Basil laughed loudly. "Only it won't be us dancing."

"Thanks, but I've got a busy day tomorrow."

"Jesus, Lucien, what happened to you? Under the thumb or what?"

I gave him a tight smile and squashed the longing to punch his shiny, round, red face. "Just busy Basil."

"What's the matter?" William asked, shoulder bumping Basil. William was a prick, but I tolerated him for the contacts he sent my way.

"Lucien is going home?"

"What the fuck?" William roared. "Why? There are women, man, fucking hot women who like fucking rich men! I'm not going home until I've got laid. Amelia hasn't fucking put out since the goddamn baby was born. I'm bouncing on space hoppers."

So many times, I'd been out with them. So many times, I'd gone home, or to a hotel, with a nameless, faceless woman who just wanted to fuck. It all seemed so long ago. A different time. A different me.

"Lucien, you're such a pussy. Man-the-fuck-up and come with us." Basil chucked a couple of twenty-pound notes onto the table and haphazardly put on his coat. "I want to see some sexy fucking pussy gyrating in my face before I go home."

I hated him.

I hated that this was what my life had been before Alice. I hated that I had a brief distraction in the waitress, like with Delphine, it was made obvious that sex could be on tap, women to fuck, no questions or commitments. I had to get out of there.

I took my phone from my pocket and flicked through the notifications. Still nothing. Fuck, Alice, where are you?

Somehow, I got swept along with the crowd to a club in a Soho basement. It was the kind of club that Delphine enjoyed and one that I spent plenty of time in during the bleakest years. Anything went, whatever sordid shit a person was into, could be found in the dark corners. Dancers writhed and gyrated on the laps of drunken, rich fucks who thought they ruled the world. I stood back, accepted a whiskey and watched the depravity. It made me feel sick.

Once, yes, I would have been part of it, choosing a woman to take home and fuck. Now however, this scene was not who I was, and I wished I'd stayed home and not put myself in a situation that could lose me Alice.

William chose a dancer and sat back on the leather sofa, his face twisted into a perverted leer and the woman began to move in his lap. Touching wasn't allowed but the security and the dancers turned a blind eye if there enough cash to make it worth their while. I watched him pull out a wad of notes, no regard at all for his wife at home with a small baby and had to cough away bile that reached my throat. Far too late, I put my glass down on a table and left the club.

I was too over that shit to be there a moment longer.

I wanted Alice. I wanted the calmness she brought to my life and the peace I felt when she was near. Even fleeting moments of lust for someone else couldn't take away what I felt for her. She was my everything. I could never, and would never, do anything to fuck it up because I loved her.

I'd never loved anyone like I loved Alice, not even Isabelle.

She was brave, feisty, sexy, clever and so beautiful that she dazzled me. In a life so dark and filled with despair and self-loathing, Alice had brought the sun. She had brought me back to life.

One day I would marry Alice, and for the first time since I'd woken, I had a smile on my face.

ALICE

"Hey," I said quietly down the phone. "It's me, did I wake you?" It was the middle of the night, but I was struggling to sleep. My mind was whirring with the information I'd read and re-read until I was almost word perfect. I'd drunk my way through the miniature vodka followed by the wines, and I was feeling fuzzy headed and worn out. I'd certainly look the part of a stressed PhD student, even if I did forget everything I'd learned.

"No, not at all, I've just got in?" Lucien was slurring a little but not enough to make me worried.

"Been anywhere nice." I shifted on the bed and wrapped the duvet tighter around myself.

"Out with the boys." I could hear the grimace. "It was a wasted evening, I had nothing in common with any of them anymore."

"No?"

"I had no idea what a lack of respect they had for anyone, and that was me once, before you. Thank fuck for you."

The smile shone from me. Once so unable to share his feelings, now there was no holding him back. My heart skipped inside my chest, dancing a merry dance against my ribs.

"Oh?" I said suggestively.

"Yeah." Lucien sighed and I could imagine him running his hands through his hair. "Honestly Alice, they're fucking dicks, splashing the cash with no cares as though the country isn't heading for the shit tip, cheating on their wives with lap dancers, honestly, I had no idea until tonight."

"Lap dancers?"

"Fuck, not me. The only person I want dancing in my lap is you, not some disease-ridden tramp." I could hear him shudder. "I used to be just like them, Alice. Arrogant, blasé and just a total cunt..."

"Lucien!"

"But they are, Alice! Rich cunts who don't give a shit." Lucien went quiet and I wondered if he'd fallen asleep.

"Lucien?"

"I'm here. I don't want this life anymore Alice. I'm tired of it. I don't want to do what I do, I just want some peace. I've filled my

144

life with work, casual women and whiskey since Isabelle left and I'm tired of it. I've got more money than I could ever spend, and I think I might just sell the company and live off what I've got. The rat race seems too fast now. There is nothing to inspire me to keep going and keep fighting to win business that I don't want anymore."

"You want to sell the business?" I sat bolt upright. "Really? But you've worked so hard to get it where it is."

"Yes," he said slowly, "yes I have but it was to hide the emptiness. I don't feel empty anymore, and if I can find Hettie the final missing piece will be in place. I've changed, Alice. My priorities have changed, and work doesn't come into that, not anymore."

"Changed how?" I held my breath.

"Changed because I'd rather spend twelve hours a day with you than I would sitting behind a desk making money that I don't need."

"You would?" I squeaked, "really?"

"Well, I couldn't do nothing, I could work for you."

"Oh, God no!"

Lucien laughed loudly. "You don't think I could make a good coffee and file papers?"

"Not for me! Oh hell, I'd get nothing done, and unlike you I don't have the option to give up work..."

"You could."

I lay back down and cuddled the pillow, balancing the phone on my ear. "No, I couldn't. I still have things I'd like to achieve, and I can't do that if I gave up work. You could always run a coffee shop if you wanted to make coffee all day."

The phone went silent and I wondered what he was thinking.

"Did you have a lap dance?" I asked, biting down hard on my lip and praying the honest answer was no.

"No. I had a mouthful of whiskey and came home. I told you, my priorities have changed, I've changed, that life has been and gone."

"Ok."

"You don't believe me?" Lucien asked softly.

"It's just..."

"I'm not who I was when you met me, Alice. You changed me. I wouldn't risk you for all the lap dances in the universe. Not for a minute. I told you, I'm going to marry you. I only need one woman to dance for me, and that's you. Forever."

"Really?"

"Really." Lucien sounded tired, weary as though the fight had gone from him. I wondered how he would really feel if he knew what I was going to do tomorrow, and the risk it carried. He loved me, I knew that, but I was playing with fire that could burn out of control, taking with it every last hope of Lucien reuniting with Henrietta and leaving nothing behind but ashes.

Fuck. I was terrified. I wanted to tell him, to have him reassure me that what I was doing was the right thing, that he wouldn't stop loving me if I got it wrong, but I couldn't say it. I couldn't ask that of him. He would have to make a promise that he wouldn't be able to keep and Lucien carried enough on his shoulders, he didn't need that too.

"What are you doing tomorrow?" He asked yawning.

"Just stuff." I said, crossing my fingers.

"Secret stuff?"

"It seems so." I replied.

"Just be careful…"

"I won't let you down." I said quickly, "I promise."

"That's not what I meant, Alice. I meant you be careful. Don't take any risks that could, I don't know, get you hurt or something. I'm not there to protect you and Jean-Claude…well, I just don't know what he is capable of."

"Lucien, I will be fine, I promise. John is here and as soon as I have something to tell you, I will tell you."

"I know." Lucien said softly, "I know you will. I miss you Alice."

"I miss you too."

"And you know…" He said, sounding like the Lucien I knew, "I really, really need a fuck."

"Soon." I whispered.

"I'll hold you to that, dirty girl."

"Good night, Lucien." I said, the term he used hitting me straight in the pussy. I was a dirty girl. I was his dirty girl.

"Good night, dirty girl."

Lucien ended the call and my surroundings were plunged into silence. Earlier so tired, my body was wide awake and yearning, and as my fingers sought the silken spot between my legs, the room became filled with the sounds of my pleasure.

ALICE

I was shaking so badly that I'd spilled coffee down myself and knocked my fruit juice over the table. The hotel waiter looked at me with concern, and I gave him a tight smile, but it didn't seem to appease him. Perhaps I looked as close to a nervous breakdown as I felt.

I must have been mad to willingly take a risk so huge. I'd read everything John had given me until I knew it off by heart, it gave me something to do when the sleep I desperately needed refused to come, but I was far from confident that I could pull it off. I thought about Lucien and the trust he'd put in me, and how difficult it must have been for him to have gone back to London, not knowing anything.

Shit, shit, shit.

I waited while my breakfast table was re-laid, keeping one hand in my pocket, wrapped tightly around the laminated card that would allow me entry into one of the most secure rehabilitation facilities in Switzerland. At least, I hoped it would. I had no idea at all if it would open the door, but I'd know soon enough, possibly when the police arrived to incarcerate me forever.

What the fuck was I doing?

When the table was laid, I sat down and offered an apology for my clumsiness. The waiter brought me over a fresh coffee and juice and handed me the breakfast menu. The letters swirled in front of my eyes, blurring until the page turned grey. Beads of sweat dropped from my forehead and my heart beat so wildly I thought I was going to pass out.

"Miss Addison, are you alright?" The waiter asked, crouching beside me and taking my elbow.

"May I have some water please?" I gasped, clutching my hand to my stomach.

"Certainly." He gestured to a commis waiter who brought over a glass decanter of iced water.

"Thank you." I whispered as my waiter poured me a glass. It was cold enough to give me an icy headache but seemed to calm the racing beat of my heart until I could breathe again.

148

"Do you need a Doctor, Miss Addison?" His accent deepened with the worry in his voice. He looked as though he wished to be anywhere except with the crazy version of me.

"No, no thank you." I shook my head. "I'm alright, really. Just low blood sugar or something, perhaps I need some food?"

"Of course, Madam." He didn't look convinced but swiftly laid the napkin across my lap and waited while I looked at the menu. The words had stopped swimming, but my stomach felt too raw for much food. I ordered what I thought my stomach would accept but knew I would likely leave most of it. I sipped my coffee, adding an extra sugar to give me an immediate boost. It was too sweet, but the repetitive action of drinking it calmed my mind. Today would be ok, because it had to be. The pass would work because everyone had a price, John was very sure about that. Nothing could go wrong because Lucien had to find his daughter, he deserved to, the ghosts of the past needed to be buried.

I sent silent prayers to the universe that my one chance at finding a piece of the puzzle would prove fruitful and I would know at least one answer. What happened the night Ottoline died.

Lucien had to know the truth because it had slowly been eating away at his soul since the accident. I wanted to pull him back from the demons that claimed him every night, that made him scream with terror as he relived Ottie's death over and over. Lucien said that I kept them at bay, but I didn't, not always, even if he was unaware of the cries in his sleep, I heard every single one and they tore at my heart with ragged fingers.

My text alert went off and I reached into my canvas university tote bag for it.

'*Morning*' Lucien messaged. '*Did you sleep ok?*'

I sighed. Another lie to tell, another hiding the truth from someone I loved. It took me back to the beginning of our relationship, the 'agreement' which became one lie after another to my friends, hiding what I was doing, mostly because I was ashamed that I was nothing more than a submissive fuck. It didn't feel right to lie anymore.

149

'*Like a log*' There it was, the lie, out there in the world for him to see. The face I saw in the mirror this morning was testament to the endless hours lying awake as the world slept around me. '*You?*'

'*Yeah, I think so. Missed you though. What are you doing today?*'

No, don't ask me, Lucien. Don't make me lie. '*Just a couple of things.*'

'*Have you heard from John?*'

'*Yes.*' I replied, thankful to have a truth to tell. '*He's following up on some leads, the team are watching Jean-Claude. Stop worrying!*'

'*I'll stop when I know what you've been up to*'

Crap. The icy hand gripped my stomach until I wanted to vomit. I was facing the end of my relationship if I got today wrong and I absolutely could not imagine my life without Lucien in it. It was unbearable after Paris, so much so that I wasn't sure I would survive with my mental health intact. It would be so much worse this time that I wasn't sure I would survive it at all.

'*I will tell you, Lucien, I promise. Please just trust me.*'

'*Always.*'

That was a promise he may not have been able to keep.

'*I love you.*' I replied. '*So much.*'

'*I love you too.*'

I put my phone back in the bag and picked up the coffee cup with trembling hands. The waiter brought the food I'd ordered to my table but when I looked down at it, the nausea rose so quickly I was forced to run to the ladies' room where I dry-heaved over the toilet. I'd known fear before, but this was alienating me from my whole body until not one limb coordinated with the other.

I was never going to get through today.

I couldn't be a tree at secondary school, how the fuck was I going to pull off the role of a lifetime convincingly, without attracting suspicion?

I sat down on the floor of the cubicle and rocked slowly back and forth, my mind empty of everything but the crippling panic that was consuming me, until the world went black.

150

ALICE

I must have only passed out for a few seconds as my coffee was still hot when I made my way stiffly back to the restaurant. I felt like my brain had had a reboot while I was unconscious, and now everything had become so much focused. My mission was clear, and I wasn't about to fail.

It was surprising how ravenous I was, and I literally inhaled my food. When I stood up, it was with a confidence that squared my shoulders and lengthened my back. Everything John had given me was running like a data programme behind my eyes, I could see every word, every minute detail that would enable me to pass any test I was given. The confidence lasted until I got off the bus and stood outside the hospital. Then my courage failed, and I felt my knees begin to buckle. *You can do this, Alice. You can.*

The entry panel lit up like a Christmas tree when I approached it with my laminated pass in my outstretched hand. It was the moment of truth, would it open or would I have to run like hell? My heart was thrashing against my ribs and as I inhaled, the breath caught in my throat. *Oh my God. Oh my fucking...* I was about to dance with the Devil and I had no idea of the steps. What was I doing? What the fuck was I doing?

The world swam in front of my eyes as I held the pass up to the scanner. *Please work, please open, please, please, please.* The scanner went back and forth along the barcode on the pass and by some miracle the door opened. I gripped the tote bag in my hand and walked through the automatic door to be greeted by a receptionist.

"Hello." I said, walking up to the desk. "I'm Holly Jones, Dr Zeldig is expecting me."

"Ah, yes, Miss Jones. Welcome. Please take the elevator to the third floor. I will let Dr Zeldig know you're here." She lifted the phone receiver and put it to her ear whilst pointing to the lift. "Third floor."

I nodded and walked across the reception, the heels of my newly purchased shoes clicking on the tiles. It was very calming, creams and greens, with muted paintings on the walls that added to the feeling that I was somewhere soothing. I'd imagined that institutions were more stark and medical-looking, with padded cells and straight jackets hanging from the walls. This was more like the entrance to a spa with pots of deep green plants dotted around and, beside the lift, a vase filled with scented flowers. If one was going to go mad, this was the place to be.

I re-read my notes in the lift. Dr Zeldig, two times PhD in psychiatric medicine, leading academic in psychiatric rehabilitation – I hope I'd remembered enough of what John had given me because with that level of intellect and specialism, I wouldn't be able to blag anything.

The lift opened to a floor painted yellow. It was a soft, spring colour that probably meant something significant although I had no idea what. I walked out onto the carpeted floor and walked towards the double doors in front of me. Like the front door, it had a buzzer and a panel for my pass. I blew out a deep breath, willed the spots in front of my eyes to go, and held the pass up. There was a click and a beep, then the doors opened, and I walked through into a short corridor, another door facing me. The panel had a red light on it that, until the doors behind me had closed securely, didn't change to green. I waited, with breath held, then held the pass up. The door panel clicked and beeped, then let me into the passageway.

So far so good.

I heard footsteps and swallowed hard. Test number three was coming with a quickened pace along the corridor to my right. I turned to smile willing my trembling hands to cease. Dr Zeldig came towards me, hand outstretched, a natural smile welcoming me.

"Miss Jones?" She asked. "I'm Stella Zeldig, I'm delighted you're joining us today."

"Pleased to meet you, Stella, I'm Holly. Thank you for having me here."

"You're very welcome. I hope you find your visit with us helpful for your studies. I had a fine letter of recommendation for you."

Dr Zeldig guided me past a series of offices and treatment rooms, chatting lightly to me as we walked. I had free reign, she said, to go anywhere and look at anything, but to keep my door pass firmly out of sight. Stella took me into her office and gave me a lanyard for my pass, that needed to be tucked under my clothes.

"Most of our residents are here voluntarily," she said, "they're suffering with mental health issues and have come here to make sense of it all. Others are here because they are a danger to themselves and others. They are the ones who are in our care because they have such complex needs that this is the safest place for them to be. I have high hopes that because we will rehabilitate them gently, they will eventually go home. We try and integrate all our clients at meals times and on the evenings when we have arranged entertainment here, but it doesn't always prove successful."

She gestured for me to sit in the chair that faced the desk and crossed to a coffee pot. "May I offer you coffee?

"Yes please." I scanned the room while she poured me coffee with milk and sugar as I'd asked. It was not how I imagined a psychiatrist's office to look. It was painted in a buttermilk shade of yellow with a cream carpet on the floor. In one corner there was a sofa and a comfortable chair with scatter cushions on both. Her desk was small with only a desktop computer and a phone on it, and on the walls were paintings in soft tones. It looked like someone's living room rather than the office of one of the world's leading minds.

"It's a lovely office." I said, taking the coffee from her.

Stella sat down in the desk chair and nodded. "I wanted to make it feel peaceful, so when clients came in, they would immediately be relaxed. I try and see every client once a week, but some need more attention than others. Sadly, I can't always see them in here, but we make it work for them in any way we can. It's not a prison, but they are not all free to go."

I had to hold myself back from asking all the questions that were tumbling through my mind. There was only one client I was interested in but to ask directly would have been too obvious and I was already worrying about my body language giving me away.

"Relax, Holly!" Stella laughed, "you're not on trial!"

"Sorry." I smiled and took a deep breath in. "Just a little nervous, it's a big deal to be here." She had no idea of the significance of the words but took them on face value and leaned forward.

"You too are a brilliant mind, I've seen your thesis, you come highly recommended. We wouldn't let just any student in here, nor would we ever give such unlimited access to our files but I've seen something in the work you've done, and the way you think, a little of me perhaps, when I was young and wanted to change the world, one broken mind at a time. Ask any questions you need to, the files are there for you to look at, we have a spare office for you along the hallway and the passwords are here." Stella tapped onto the keyboard of her computer and the printer on the shelf behind her whirred into life.

"Please memorise these and shred them. Some of our more complex clients would take great delight in wiping the files if they could!"

"Are any of them dangerous?" I asked, having an image of Jack Nicholson in The Shining. I had no idea about complex mental patients, nor how to fend off an aggressive crazy person.

"Sometimes." Stella admitted. "But the staff are trained to deal with difficult situations. Mostly our clients just want to get better and we have a lovely facility here for them to do just that."

We drank our coffee while Stella told me about the world-class rehabilitation centre, and the methods they used to help the patients. She was an inspiring woman, passionate and determined to make a difference which made my deception harder to swallow. Stella spent a couple of hours with me, showing me around, introducing me to the staff and finally to the small office that she had set up for me.

"All the client files are on here," she said, "but your passwords will expire in forty-eight hours, and I cannot issue more. PhD students don't normally get this sort of access and it took a lot of persuading of the board to allow you to view them, so you won't have a lot of time to get information for your study."

"It's ok." I said, "I'm grateful for this opportunity and I won't be wasting it."

"Your pass will give you access to all areas except my office and the medication suite. Only the doctors and medical nursing staff are allowed in there."

"Do you have medical doctors here."

"I'm qualified to give medicine, as are the senior nursing staff, we have one duty doctor here all the time and one of Zurich's most senior doctor's volunteers here."

"Oh?"

"Yes, we're very lucky. He's a fantastic doctor and has personally been responsible for one of our patients. He volunteers here in exchange for her treatment. It's a very sad case, the woman in question is very troubled and very, very ill medically. Her family didn't have the money for her care, so he took it on. There are some wonderful people in this world, aren't there?"

I felt sick to my stomach. "There certainly is." I smiled, as my mouth filled with acid.

"I suppose that's why we all follow this path, to make a difference." Stella patted my arm. "It has been a great pleasure to welcome you here. Enjoy your time and please, ask any questions. If the staff don't know the answer, come and find me, I'll be very happy to help you. It's not often we entertain the next great mind."

Stella left me in the small office. I eyed the computer and slowly walked around the desk to sit down. From the corner of my eye I saw the red light of the security camera flash as it picked up my movements. I tried to be blasé, pulling out my tablet, notebook and water bottle, placing them on the table. Thank god John had given me a device that would deactivate the security camera for long enough that I could print any evidence I found. As I delayed logging onto the computer to avoid suspicion, I wondered how much I could find out in forty-eight hours, and would it be enough?

ALICE

Well, there was no patient in this facility called Clarisse Benoit. Fuck.

I leaned back in the chair and folded my hands behind my head. Jean-Claude had her here, that much was definite, but I couldn't ask which patient was his without attracting attention of the wrong kind. I trolled through the patient list once more, noting the floors and wings that were within the facility. The most secure patients were on the top two floors and I wondered if that was where she had been placed, and if so, why?

I still couldn't figure out why she was here. There was something I wasn't seeing and even when I looked at every conceivable reason why she would be here, all I came up with was a big, black hole of nothing. I exited the programme and walked out of the office, my personal belongings in a money wallet under my clothes. I knew I wasn't supposed to have any recording devices on me whilst in the hospital but if I did find Clarisse, and she had something to say, I needed proof of the conversation.

"Ah Holly!" Dr Zeldig was along the corridor standing in front of the first set of double doors with a man that I knew instantly was Jean-Claude Benoit. I fixed a smile on my face, hoping it reached my eyes or at least, looked as natural as it could in front of the man who had taken Lucien's life. "Let me introduce you to Dr Jean-Claude Bissett. Dr Bissett is Zurich's leading surgeon and we are very pleased that he helps us here. Dr Bissett, this is Holly Jones, PhD Psychiatry under Dr Robbins tutelage. She is with us as part of her thesis."

"Delighted to meet you Miss Jones." Jean-Claude said smoothly. "Welcome to Zurich."

I wanted to punch him in his chiselled jaw. Instead I smiled and held out my hand, which he took in his warm, dry palm. "I am very pleased to meet you Dr Bissett. Dr Zeldig has told me much about you."

"All good I hope?" He said lightly. Jean-Claude was handsome, not in a Lucien kind of way, more like an aged member of a boy band. Sandy hair peppered with grey and strange blue/green eyes that seemed more in tune with an alien hybrid than a Frenchman. His accent was barely noticeable, just the odd inflection on a word but there was something sinister behind the easy smile. I didn't trust him. Even if I didn't know what I did about him, I would never have trusted him. There was a coldness behind the calm manner and the way he studied me with a smooth smile on his face, made him look shifty, and made me feel uneasy. The sooner I could get out of there, the better.

"Dr Zeldig tells me you volunteer here, Dr Bissett." I said, casually taking my hand back. "That's a very generous way to spend your free time, I can't imagine you have much of it to give away?"

"Not as much as my fiancée would like!" He laughed, showing perfectly white teeth. "My job and family life don't go so well together."

"I suppose it doesn't."

"Do you have a family Miss Jones?" Jean-Claude asked.

"No, not yet." I shrugged. "Still single and focusing on my work, once my PhD research is completed, then I may just look at the sorry state of my social life!" Stella and Jean-Claude joined in with my laughter.

"We all have a sorry social life in this field," Stella said, "it comes with the territory." She glanced at her watch. "Jean-Claude, Holly, do excuse me, I have a meeting to attend." I smiled at her and watched Jean-Claude lean in and kiss her on each cheek.

"May I walk you to where you are headed?" He asked me. "I have to pay a short visit to my patient."

"Thank you, yes please. I am heading to," I feigned looking at the list on the paper in my hand. "Floor five."

"Likewise." Jean-Claude gestured along the corridor and we walked along to the lift. "Why this field?" He asked, sounding interested.

I gave him the background that John had invented for me, academic parents, a first-class honours degree, a Master's in psychology, employment in psychiatric units and finally the doctorate. There was nothing in my tone or manner that would have made anyone question anything I said, it was word-perfect, plausible and could easily be followed up online, John had left no gap anywhere.

"What about you?" I asked, "how did you come to volunteer here? Dr Zeldig tells me you are a brilliant surgeon."

"That's nice to know." Jean-Claude said as the lift opened. He held out his hand to allow me to exit the lift first. "I had a patient who was in a very bad way, she needed the security and safety of a unit, this one was perfect but her family were poor and they wouldn't hear of me paying for it, so I made a deal with the board, my medical services for her care. It works. She is happy and I am relieved that she is safe." He smiled. "Some sad souls are too much of a danger to themselves to be in the outside world. It's tragic."

"Yes," I said, "it is, but that is why we do what we do, whatever the sacrifice to our personal lives. Your family must be very proud of what you do here."

"Yes, they are."

"You have children?" I asked casually looking down at the paper in my hand, then around the corridor to the numbers on the wall.

"Yes, one. A daughter. Grace. She is fifteen now, I can't say she is that enamoured with me, I confess to being stricter than a teenager would like!" Jean-Claude laughed. "It may pay off one day."

"It generally does." I agreed. "I recall my father being strict, but now I'm glad, I wouldn't have been doing what I do, if he hadn't been." My mind was whirring. That was why John couldn't find Hettie, she had a different name. "Thank you for escorting me here. I won't take up any more of your time, but it was a pleasure to meet you." The lie dripped easily from my tongue. I waved the paper and continued, "and here begins my research!"

"Good luck, and if you need anything," Jean-Claude took a card from his pocket, "just let me know, I'd be delighted to help."

"You're too kind." I said, taking the card and glancing down on it. "Thank you."

Jean-Claude nodded and walked down the corridor, not looking back. I pretended to study the paper, one eye on his movements, then slowly, carefully, I followed him, being sure to stay back, keeping the paper in front of me as though I was finding my way. I watched him pause outside of a room and then walk in. I casually walked past the room and saw him taking a chair beside a woman who was sleeping on a single bed. He gently roused her but as she woke, fear flooded her face and I knew instantly that I'd found Clarisse.

LUCIEN

"So, what are my options?" I asked. My lawyer, Charles, shifted in his seat and took a big breath in. I was being impulsive, and it made Charles nervous. I'd been impulsive before, plenty of times, and Charles had never once looked at me the way he was looking at me now.

"Well, you can sell, Lucien, you own the business, it would be easy to do so, there are no loose strings anywhere, no board, but what you're suggesting, well, you can't. Isabelle would still be able to claim half."

"We've been separated for ten years, Charles. Ten." I held up splayed fingers. "Ten years, not ten fucking minutes."

"I realise that, but there has been nothing legally noted about a separation, so, in the eyes of the law, you're still married, she'll get half. The only way to ensure that she gets nothing, is to sign the divorce papers."

"You know I can't do that." I said, slumping back into my chair. "Not while she's keeping Hettie from me. There has to be another option."

"There is. Keep the business, sort your private life and when that's done, sell. You have plenty of time, Lucien, it doesn't all have to be done right now. Why sell anyway? You have one of London's most successful corporations, why throw in the towel?"

"I just don't want to do it anymore, Charles. I'm tired. Tired of the constant stress, tired of the fucking projections of doom and gloom, I want to have some time off…"

"So, take time off Lucien, don't sell your company!"

"It looks like I can't anyway," I shrugged crossly. "Not if I want to keep Isabelle and Jean-fucking-Claude away from my money. Christ alive why is it so goddamn difficult?"

"I don't know mate, but until you give Isabelle what she wants, it looks like you're stuck."

"Is there anything in there," I gestured at the divorce papers on the desk between us, "that we can get her with?"

"No, not that I've seen on first glance, but I'll take it all away to read."

160

"Can she really keep Hettie from me?"

Charles scratched his cheek and took a while to speak. "As it stands, Lucien, at aged fifteen Hettie's feelings would be taken into consideration. If she wants to be adopted by Jean-Claude, the courts would very likely agree. She's old enough to decide for herself which makes it very hard to object to and, if Jean-Claude had the real records somewhere, and Isabelle decided to use them as proof that you're an unfit father, you'd be completely screwed and very likely end up in jail."

I sat upright. "What if I could prove my innocence."

"That would be a whole different ball game, Lucien." Charles leaned forward in his seat. "Can you?"

"Alice is onto something."

Charles' face fell. "I hoped, for a moment, that you had something concrete."

"Not yet." I massaged my temples. My headaches were getting worse as the days without Alice merged into each other. I was struggling to have more than a few hours of sleep and couldn't concentrate on anything for more than a couple of minutes. Alice had gone dark and even my usual methods of finding her were failing to track her down. Charles looked at me steadily and said nothing.

"I suppose I just have to wait." I said eventually.

"It looks that way." Charles packed the papers into his leather bag and stood up. "When your PI has come up with the goods, then we can revisit it all, but honestly Lucien, now is not the time to be selling your business, nor doing anything that'll get you arrested."

"So you've told me." I muttered, nodding across the office to Carol who was loitering outside the door. At my nod she pushed the glass door and came to escort Charles downstairs. I stood up to shake his hand and we said our goodbyes. I sensed he had more to say but whatever it was, he refrained from speaking and merely turned his back to walk out with Carol.

I was fucked. Completely fucked. Without a divorce there was no chance of moving my life forward with Alice, and if I did divorce, I lost Hettie permanently.

I was trapped in a steaming pile of shit. I looked out of the window at the pouring rain. There had to be answers somewhere because nothing could stay hidden forever. I wondered for the umpteenth time what Alice was up to, but the phone had stayed silence and even John hadn't updated me. I didn't know how long I could sit in London for, just waiting for someone to give me back control of my life. It was driving me fucking crazy. I took the tatty piece of paper, with the address of Ottoline's grave on it, from my wallet and stared at it. Why was Alice so convinced that I didn't kill her when everything pointed at me? What the fuck was she doing in Zurich and, more importantly, I thought, glaring at my quiet phone, where the fuck was she?

ALICE

I was so far in over my head I couldn't see my surroundings. It was all very well to blag everyone with the details John had given me, but to blag the seriously mentally ill patient who was talking to me, was a different matter altogether and the guilt twisted my head in a vice. I had Lucien's face firmly in my mind, the very clear reason as to why I was there, but as I chatted to the patient, making notes as any PhD student would have, my conscience screamed at me. My intentions were good but fuck me, my actions were unspeakable.

I shot a quick glance to the corridor. Jean-Claude was talking to one of the senior nurses, his hands moving rapidly as he spoke. He signed some paperwork on the clipboard the nurse was holding and turned quickly, leaving the ward through the security doors, towards the lift. My heart began to pound so quickly in my chest that my head spun, and I had to grip the sides of my chair to remain upright. Now was my chance, possibly my only chance. I had no idea if my card would even get me back in tomorrow.

"Thank you for speaking to me." I told the lady sitting opposite me. I wasn't sure she'd heard me, her eyes were darting from side to side as though she were in a trance. I gathered up my papers and excused myself, watching for the nurses who were doing their rounds.

"How are you getting on Holly?" One of them asked as she handed the eye-spinning lady some medication.

"Almost done here." I said smiling, feeling a rib metaphorically break under the beating from my heart.

"Already?"

"I have to try and see all the patients but it's a big unit and they've only allowed me two days."

"Oh!"

I nodded lightly. "It's better than nothing." The nurse turned her attention from me, and I took the chance to leave the common room. I walked as confidently as I could manage to Clarisse's room and gently tapped on the glass pane in the door.

She was curled up in a ball on the single bed that was pushed against the wall of her room. One hand raised slightly, and I took it as permission to enter. I had the small Dictaphone from John in my money wallet, that I'd hidden inside a box of tampons to avoid having it confiscated. Fuck, I was actually doing this. My hands were shaking so much I could barely close the door behind me and when I walked over to the upright easy chair beside the bed, it was on legs made of lead.

"Hello, Florence," I said gently, using the name listed on the door. "My name is Holly"

"My name is Clarisse." She muttered in English, accented with French inflections. "Why does everyone insist on calling me Florence. That is the name he gave me, why won't you people listen?"

I clicked the Dictaphone. "Clarisse. I am recording this conversation. Do you give me permission?"

"Do what you like, the others do. He does."

"Can you give me your permission?"

"Yes, you have my permission. It's nice to be asked for a change."

"Why do they call you Florence?" I asked. My mouth was so dry that my tongue was clicking against my teeth.

"He called me Florence."

"Who?"

"Jean-Claude, my husband. Although he'll tell you he has another name and that I am insane." Clarisse shook her head and a tear rolled down her cheek. I moved closer to her, handing her a tissue from the small, square box on the table.

"Are you insane?"

She sighed deeply. "The drugs they give me here, prescribed by him, were making me feel insane. Before it all happened, I was normal, happy, content with my life. But he had to keep me silent, so I got imprisoned in here. Who would doubt the word of a mighty doctor, saviour of the people?" Clarisse coughed harshly and when she wiped her mouth, blood was on the tissue. "He's getting his wish after all."

"His wish?"

"I'm dying. Lung cancer. Ironic really, as I've never smoked. Not even in here, where there is nothing to do but speak to crazy people, take medication and stare out of the window at the world I long to be part of. Everyone smokes in here, they don't know they're doing it half the time…There was a twisted pleasure when he told me that my diagnosis was terminal. I see nothing of my husband in the man he has become."

She sounded so normal yet here she was telling her inner most thoughts to a total stranger and I began to panic that I'd got it very, very wrong. What if Lucien had been right, what if he'd killed Ottie and they had run from him to keep Hettie safe. What if I didn't know him at all and I was putting myself through this deception for nothing?

"I am very sorry." I whispered, "I cannot imagine how you must feel knowing this."

"Who are you?" She suddenly asked, moving on the bed to face me. "Who are you really?"

I felt guilt cross my features and twisted my face into a smile. "I'm Holly, I'm here for PhD research."

"No, you're not."

I nodded, grinning. "I definitely am."

"You're not." Clarisse coughed again and said, "I've not taken my medication in weeks. Weeks." She waited, watching me, while I digested her words. There was a long pause as I tried to think of something to say. "Well, Holly, if you were really who you say you are, you'd have run off to tell the nurses and they would be in here doing bloods and swabs and all sorts by now. So, I'll ask you again, who are you?"

"I'm who I said I was." I replied calmly. "I'm doing a PhD on psychiatric care and I was lucky enough to have been allowed in here to do my research."

"You are a very good liar, but a liar nonetheless." Clarisse sat up on her bed, grimacing as she did and pulled herself up to standing. She was a tiny, gaunt woman with sunken cheeks and pallid skin but there was a fire in her eyes that was at odds with the disease that was claiming her. Clarisse shuffled to the shelf on the wall behind the chair and took down at CD case, inside of which were tablets of all sizes and colours. "See, my medication. So, what are you going to do about that?"

165

It felt as though she'd had me up against a wall with a gun to my head.

"Nothing."

"I thought as much."

"What are you going to do?" I asked nervously.

"Nothing." Clarisse replied. "I will merely wait until you tell me why you are here pretending to be someone you're not. And then I'll wait for you to tell me how you will get me out of here, because I am not dying in this place."

I could outrun her and with luck I could be out of the building before she'd managed to walk out of the room, but I sensed that wasn't her plan. She was cunning and had a great spirit, but she was also broken and frightened.

"My name is Alice and I am in love with Lucien Ross." I told her.

Clarisse reached for my arm. Her hand felt papery against my skin and I stood to help her sit back down on her bed. She coughed violently so I poured her a cup of water and waited until she could speak.

"Lucien Ross? Then, my dear Alice, I have a story to tell you."

ALICE

I leaned in. Clarisse nodded at the Dictaphone and said, "you need to make sure there is plenty of room on that."

"Why?"

"Because Lucien Ross is the reason I am here."

"I don't understand." I said, my mouth going even more dry. Did Lucien put her in here? He couldn't have, he didn't know where any of them were. I was momentarily distracted by a nurse walking past, talking on a phone. He didn't appear to notice me sitting in the chair.

"I need to be quick, they'll be in soon." Clarisse said. She coughed to clear her voice. "My name is Clarisse Benoit, wife of Jean-Claude Benoit who is now presenting himself as Jean-Claude Bissett. I am of sound mind, despite what my husband wants everyone to believe and according to my husband, my cancer diagnosis is aggressive, so I won't live much longer. Therefore, I have no reason to lie and that is the reason I am in here. You see, my husband killed Ottoline Ross."

Time stopped. I don't think I even took a breath. "What?" I asked in a shocked whisper. "What did you say." The Dictaphone whirred softly on the table and I leaned to check it had plenty of tape.

"Jean-Claude Benoit killed Ottoline Ross. Not on purpose, he wasn't a bad man, not then at least, but, yes, he was the reason it happened."

"How?" How could I prove that this wasn't the ranting of a mad, dying woman, locked up in an institution for the best part of a decade. How could I take my evidence to the police and have it taken seriously? I was in stormy water so violent that there was no way I could swim out, and if what Clarisse was saying was true, how could I tell Lucien when a Doctor could easily dismiss it as the rantings of a dying woman intent on reaping havoc. I'd opened pandoras box and I had totally blown everything.

"He was having an affair with Isabelle Ross. The night Ottoline died, he and Isabelle were trying to find a way of being together."

"How do you know this?"

167

"I saw them. I knew about the affair, of course I did. Secrets don't stay buried and with the sexual attraction between them, it was so obvious that I was surprised that Lucien didn't know too. He was so blind to her, he worshipped the very ground she walked on. That night…"

"Hello, Holly, I wondered where you were. I wanted to know if you'd like to join some of the senior staff and I for lunch?" Stella had knocked on the door and let herself in, not waiting for an answer. "Hello Florence, you're up!"

"It's Clarisse." She muttered.

"Of course," Stella said, beaming. "About half an hour Holly?"

"That would be lovely," I said nodding with a smile on my face, "thank you."

"Not too much longer with Florence, Holly, she gets very tired."

"*She* can hear you." Clarisse said crossly.

"Now, now, don't go upsetting yourself." Stella excused herself and the door banged behind her.

Clarisse coughed again and her frail frame shook. I helped her lie back down in her bed and covered her with the sheet.

"The night Ottoline died we'd been entertaining many friends at home. Lucien and Isabelle were there, they were our best friends, it would have been odd had they not been although, it was a few days before that evening when I'd discovered what Jean-Claude and Isabelle were up to." Grief flooded Clarisse's face and my heart hurt for her.

"Was Lucien drunk?"

"No."

"Then how did Ottie die?"

"Jean-Claude put a sedative in Lucien's drink. It was supposed to knock him out for a few hours so they could have that time together. Jean-Claude gave me one too, but mine worked. Everyone just assumed I'd had too much to drink, everyone else was drunk, we'd been drinking all day, the children were being looked after by the nanny we'd hired for the day…"

"And Lucien."

"He was the only sober one there. The sedative hit when he was driving home and he crashed the car."

168

"He has blamed himself for ten years." I said, tears spilling from my eyes. "Ten years. It has eaten him up and he nearly died because of his guilt. All this time. All the hurt and guilt and grief. Isabelle took Hettie…"

"I know. It was just before I got sectioned. Jean-Claude admitted everything, he was drunk, naturally, it was a regular occurrence, but I'd recorded the conversation onto a tape, I wanted evidence that I could use to divorce him. He didn't want a scandalous divorce, of course, it wouldn't have been good for the great pillar of society to have been caught cheating. So, I set up the tape and somehow, we got onto the conversation about Lucien and he told me how and why. I hid the tape and called the police, but he was so believable when they showed up, they took me instead. He took everything from me. I wanted to have children, we'd been talking about it for months in the run up to Ottie's death, but that isn't possible now." Tears fell down her cheeks, dampening the pillow under her head. "I was desperate to be a mother and he took that from me. I will probably be in here until my last breath and Jean-Claude will have no reason to look over his shoulder anymore. He can't get away with it, he just can't."

"I'll do everything I can to get you out of here, Clarisse. I will try, I promise."

"I don't want to die in here, I want to go home."

"Where is home?"

"It's a small village about forty miles south from where our Chateau is. Lucien will know where the village is. It overlooks the sea and I'd like to think that my family are still there. That is where I want to be. Please get me there. Please."

"I will do whatever I can do, you have my word."

"Take that," she nodded at the Dictaphone, "and get out of here before they find it. It wasn't Lucien, Alice, it was Jean-Claude. The evidence for that is in the Chateau." Clarisse spoke the address clearly into the Dictaphone. It wasn't far from where Ottie was buried. "The tape is still there."

"Where?" I asked, packing everything but the recorder into my bag. "Where is the tape?"

Clarisse told me where I could find it. I leaned over and wrapped my arms around her thin frame. "I will do what I can." I whispered and lightly kissed her cheek. "You have my word."

"Go." She replied, her tired voice barely audible. "Go before they find you still here."

"Bye Clarisse."

She was asleep before I'd packed the Dictaphone back into the wallet beneath my clothes. Careful to not draw attention to myself, I walked as casually as I could manage from the secure suite to the lift. I stopped at the office to get my tablet and notebook, then pushing the button in the lift for the ground floor I prayed to the heavens no one would get into the lift and question me. A deity was listening because when the lift door opened, it was the ground floor. I used my pass to release the security doors and without speaking to the receptionist I walked from the building to the street.

As soon as I was as far away from the hospital as I could get, I pulled out my phone. "John?" I said when he finally answered, "I need to see you. Right now."

He named a hotel that would be least likely to be frequented by anyone I might have met at the hospital and I hailed a cab, giving the address, and, sinking into the seat, I squeezed my eyes shut to stop the tears. I longed to believe Clarisse, longed to be able to set Lucien free from his demons, but the story was too far-fetched and my cover was blown, I had no way of getting back into the hospital but I had to keep my promise, whatever the cost, I had to keep the promise I made.

I felt sure I'd totally screwed up and the anxious feelings began to gnaw at my stomach, like sharp teeth ripping through my flesh. What was I to do now? How could I prove she was telling the truth?

What the fuck was I to say to Lucien?

Had I just blown an irreparable hole in his search and how could I possibly make it alright?

How could Lucien forgive me if Isabelle ran again?

It was the longest cab ride of my life.

ALICE

John stared at the Dictaphone as Clarisse's voice held him completely still. He looked shocked and the more the story unfolded, the paler he became.

"Well...fuck." He said as the tape came to a stop. John shook his head in complete disbelief and bit on a nail. I said nothing as the truth began to sink in. "How can we prove this? She's in the loony bin, no-one in their right mind would take her seriously. Lucien is just as fucked as he was before. John stopped chewing his nail leaned his head in his hands. "I've been trying to resolve this case for years, but everything came up as a blank and now I think they may actually beat me."

"John." I said sharply. "Now is not the time to give up. We can sort this and this is how I think we should do it." John waited while I assembled my thoughts. "Your team can look for Grace Bisset. She has to be in Zurich, he mentioned his family not liking the time he spent away from them. He and Isabelle can't get married until Clarisse is dead, and from the looks of her that won't be long, so we have to get her out of there, even if we kidnap her."

"We can hardly do that Alice." John said crossly, "I'm a PI not an abductor of crazy people."

"I'm not suggesting we abduct her, for God's sake, we'd be arrested, and all this would have been for nothing. Before we do anything, we need to go to their chateau, the tape is there, it has Jean-Claude's confession on it, without that we have nothing at all, and he will get away with it.

"Do you know where the Chateau is?"

"Yes."

"Then we need to leave now. Do you want to tell Lucien?" John asked me.

"Not until we have that confession." I sighed. "What a fucking mess this is, hey John. How can a person live with this deceit?"

"I couldn't, Alice. It would eat me up."

"Maybe some people just don't care. Isabelle was his prize and he was going to get her anyway he could. Do you think she knows he killed Ottie?"

171

"How can she? Would you stay with someone who killed your daughter because he wanted to get his leg over?"

"No." I replied softly. "No, I wouldn't."

"Isabelle is clever and her way of doing things has made her a huge bitch, but if you think your husband is capable of killing your child, wouldn't you have kept the remaining child safe?"

"I suppose." I looked down at my watch. "Can we get to France now?"

John picked up his laptop. Plugging the Dictaphone in, he saved the file and emailed a copy to me. Once he'd done that, he put the recording device into a secure case and turned his attention back to the keyboard. I watched him type but sat with my own thoughts, mainly of Clarisse. What sort of lowlife was he to leave her languishing in an institution where she didn't need to be? I tried to imagine her anguish, but I just couldn't, it went beyond my creativity to bring up that depth of pain that she must have felt every day since Ottie died. Jean-Claude's selfish needs destroyed so many lives that day and I wanted to see him burn for what he had done.

"Alice?" John looked up from his laptop, "If we go now, we can make the train that leaves at five. Where is your passport?"

"At my hotel."

"Pack an overnight bag, get your passport and meet me at the station by four forty-five."

"How are you going to keep it from Lucien, you have a company credit card."

"I've used mine, he'll sort me out."

"If we find nothing, John, please don't tell Lucien. I'll pay you for the tickets. This will be on me."

"He's lucky to have you Alice." John said gruffly. "I hope he knows that."

"He may not be so lucky if we end up on a wild-goose chase."

"This has been ten years of wild-goose chases, Alice. One more won't make a difference."

What if he was wrong?

I left the hotel and took a cab back to the hotel. What a day. I couldn't shake the fear that Clarisse was seriously mentally and physically ill and that she would have, by now, alerted everyone to us being here. Jean-Claude, Isabelle and Hettie could be long gone, and I would have blown it for Lucien, probably forever.

I hoped I would find the tape when we got to France otherwise, I may never be able to look Lucien in the eye again and a life without him was a desolate thought.

ALICE

John dozed for most of the train journey whilst I attempted to do some work. My new client was bombarding me with emails, Saffron was bombarding me and even Lucien added to the mix. It made my inbox look overwhelming and I wondered how I was going to get everything done in time. Lucien was far more important than anything else, but my business had been my saving grace and I had to invest far more time in it then I had of late.

I logged into the design software and began to experiment with images. It was a long journey and by the time we reached our destination I'd made some progress. Not enough, but it would keep everyone sweet for a short time. John had updates from his team in Zurich and they were keeping a close eye on Isabelle and Jean-Claude. So far, Clarisse hadn't blown my cover, but I'd no idea if that was temporary and the fear that had been dormant whilst on the train, had come back with a swift kick.

"You look pale Alice," John commented, not unkindly. "Your PI job taking its toll?"

"I was just worrying that my cover would be blown, and that Jean-Claude and Isabelle will run again. How would I ever look Lucien in the eye again?"

"My team are watching them like hawks Alice, if they try to run, we will know about it." He meant to be reassuring but there was something in his tone that made me nervous. Perhaps it was the long journey to France he'd made on a whim with me, based on the say so of someone who had an agenda, maybe it was nerves too. Who knew, John didn't give anything away, his expression barely changed.

The train slowed to a stop and the driver spoke in rapid French to the passengers who began to gather their belongings. I stood up and stretched my back, before pulling my small bag down from the overhead shelf. The hotel had been informed that I would be away for a couple of days, so my whereabouts wouldn't be noted, and I'd sent an email to the hospital from the Holly Jones account that John had set up for me so there was minimal chance of them finding me, unless they traced me back through Lucien. Shit, I'd not thought of that.

"Alice," John said, "you need to stop worrying."

"I've broken the law, I impersonated someone, I feel sick…"

"Look," he said, putting his hand onto the small of my back to guide me from the train. "I'll admit, this isn't every day stuff, but you didn't steal anything, you didn't use any of the access codes to look at files, all you did was view a patient list, which you'd be able to view at the front desk. You have done no harm Alice, none at all. Trust me, I've been doing this for years."

I nodded and climbed down the train steps. We took a taxi from outside of the station to the address Clarisse had given me. I knew the area from when I visited Ottie's grave with Lucien and I hoped to have time to take some flowers there, from Lucien, he'd appreciate that.

The taxi dropped us on the edge of the village. It was small, with three Chateaus at its borders. The smallest one was Lucien's, the largest one being Jean-Claude's. We walked through the village and followed our phone maps to get the right property. It was closed up, the shutters fixed against the windows and rust on the hinges of the door. It hadn't been visited in a long time. I rummaged through the overgrown bush, disturbing more creepy crawlies than I cared too, and found the small tin that contained the key.

"Here goes nothing." I said dryly, putting the key into the lock. I didn't expect it to turn but with force the lock clanked, and the door opened.

The building smelt dank and musty. There was dust covering every surface and discarded boots were under the window, as though the inhabitants had just run away. Which, I supposed, they had. John and I headed up the stairs to the small office off the master suite, just as Clarisse had described. I found the box beneath the floorboards, exactly where Clarisse said it would be and then John and I hurried from the Chateau, locking the door and putting the key back as we'd found it.

I'm not sure either of us took a breath until we were back in the village. I bought a small bouquet of flowers and we took the road that led away from the square towards the church. John waited while

I tidied Ottie's grave and added the fresh water to the vase. I whispered a few words to Ottie and then John called for the taxi. We were back at the station and on the sleeper train before I could really relax.

"We will need to buy a cassette player." I commented to John as we sat in the dining car. "If such a thing can still be bought."

"I have one."

"Of course you do!"

John grinned. "I have everything a PI needs, and more." He yawned. "Go and get some sleep Alice, you've had a day stranger than most, we will look at the train tomorrow."

"What will you do?" I asked.

"Follow up with the team mainly. Then sleep. I have a feeling the shit will hit the fan just as soon as we're back."

I felt my face fall. "It'll all be good, Alice." John said, "you have the makings of a fine PI!"

"I'll take that as a compliment," I grinned. "Good night John."

I left him working on his laptop and went back to my small train cabin. Sinking onto the lumpy mattress I briefly thought of Lucien before sleep took me and I drifted into a deep, dreamless sleep.

ALICE

"She wasn't lying." I muttered grimly, rubbing my eyes. We'd been back in Zurich for a couple of hours and had listened to the tape over and over, looking for any possibility it was a fake. It wasn't. It matched perfectly, everything that Clarisse had told me at the hospital. "Which also means she has been locked up in a secure facility, because of a lie, for ten years. He is despicable."

"Or scared shitless." John replied. "Which doesn't make it right, before you kill me with that death stare. You know what I mean. Ah, shit, I always know how to handle my work, always know exactly when to tell the client and how, but this time, I've no idea." John stared out of the window his eyes unfocused. Momentarily he looked lost and confused as though this case had caused the weight of the world to lie on his shoulders.

"Before we do anything, we have to know where Hettie is, then we tell Lucien and then we go to the police." I said. John blinked a few times and turned his gaze to me. "Hettie is the next piece in the puzzle and I'm worried that Isabelle will run if the police swoop in. Lucien has to see Hettie before we can do anything with that," I nodded at the tape. "And we have to somehow get Clarisse out of the facility and home to her family cottage. That's where she wants to be, and we have to make it happen, I think that will have to be Lucien's job as I'm pretty sure he'll do anything to make sure she is ok. They are both victims of Jean-Claude's actions, I wonder how he sleeps at night knowing that he destroyed two peoples' lives." I sighed, my thoughts drifting to the third person, Ottie. "So, I guess we wait for your team."

John nodded. I wondered what it must be like to have a job so valuable and de-valued such as his. He had worked for Lucien for such a long time that he was one of Lucien's most trusted people, but this case must have taken its toll. To continually find dead-ends and for every avenue to come to nothing, must affect him in some way. I wanted to ask, but John didn't strike me as the kind of person who would open up.

"I need to ring Lucien," I said. "I was supposed to tell him everything yesterday and I've left my phone switched off. I promised I'd tell him, but I still can't say anything. Shit."

"Lucien will be pissed."

"Then it's just as well I'm in Zurich."

LUCIEN

"Where the fuck have you been?" I raged down the phone to Alice. Without waiting for her to reply, I continued, "I've been worried fucking sick, I nearly got on a goddamn plane, Alice. You promised you'd phone and that was two days ago. What the fuck is going on?"

"Lucien," she replied sighing. "I'm tired. I don't need you to yell at me. Things are in hand, I had something I needed to do..."

"With John?"

"Yes."

"Are you having an affair with John?" I'm not sure why I asked but I was so fucking angry, and equally relieved that she wasn't dead in a Zurich ditch, that I was no longer feeling rational.

"What? Seriously, Lucien..."

"Don't *seriously, Lucien* me, Alice. Just don't. I've had a shit day, you vanished, your phone was switched off..."

"Sorry." Alice whispered, "I'm sorry I worried you, but I was so single-minded in what I was doing that I had to just do it. I know it's shit for you, being in London and not knowing anything and I know I probably should tell you it all but I'm so worried that we'll get it wrong and get your hopes ups for it all to be shot to shit." I could hear her voice wobble and I imagined her lovely face screwed up against the worry in her voice. She sounded like she was close to tears and the last thing I wanted to do was make her cry. I'd done enough of that.

"No, Alice, I'm sorry. I didn't mean to be angry, it was more relief than anything else. I've been going out of my mind."

"I know." I could barely hear her. "I have news, Lucien." She sounded as though telling me was not what she wanted to do. I closed my eyes and braced myself for bad news. "We have a lead on Hettie..."

"I'm coming out..." I stuffed my passport, always kept in my office drawer, into my jacket pocket and stood up so fast I knocked my chair over. It crashed and Carol looked up concerned.

"No!" Alice said quickly. "Please, Lucien, be patient for just a little longer, please. John's team are closing in and he thinks it will be a few days, if that. Please wait and just trust us, both of us want to get this right. I know you want to be here and I know that this must be killing you…probably you should be here, but so much has come out since I last spoke to you that we have to be so much more careful than before."

There was an urgency in her voice that I'd not heard before and it gave me such an overwhelming sense of hope that I almost didn't breathe. They had a lead which was closer than we'd ever been, in all the years that had passed, there had never been words uttered with such surety.

"Ok," I said finally, picking up my chair and sitting back down. "Ok, I'll take your lead on this, but Alice, if there is the slightest doubt, I'm going to be on the first plane out. If anything goes wrong it needs to be on me, not on you, do you understand?"

"Yes. It's all I've been thinking about Lucien, how much is at stake if I get things wrong. I've been in a constant state of anxiety that my hands permanently shake. I still don't know if I've fucked it up or not, and that will be absolutely on me." I heard her swallow hard and when the next words came, they were carried on a voice that broke. "Maybe I shouldn't have ever taken this from you, perhaps you should have stayed here, but Lucien I wanted to make everything right for you, because I love you so much…I am so scared I've made it worse."

"Have you?"

"I don't know."

I felt an ache in my chest, so strong that it made me dizzy. I wondered if it was what a heart-attack felt like, an icy cold fear that travelled through every organ until they all failed. I loved Alice, she'd saved me, stood up to me, excited me, turned me on so much it was a physical pain, but if this went wrong, I didn't know what it would mean. I just had to trust her and believe that it would all be alright.

"I don't know how long I can sit on the side lines for, Alice. It's all I think about."

There was a long pause. I could hear her breathing down the phone until the line went quiet and I could hear her whispering to someone, John I presumed, and eventually she said softly, "then come."

"Really?"

"Yes, and bring a kick arse lawyer and the best psychiatrist you can find."

"What? Why?"

"Just do it. I have to go, I love you." The phone line went dead and I just listened to the clicking of dead air. What the fuck did I need a lawyer or psychiatrist for? What the fuck had she found out.

"Carol?" I yelled, storming across the office. "I need you to get me the first flight out of London tomorrow for Zurich, I need Charles to be on it and the very best psychiatric doctor you can find, I don't care what it costs. Make sure they both get a room in the same hotel as Alice and I." Carol nodded and began tapping on her keyboard. "I'm going home to pack. Please cancel my appointments and I'll be back when I'm back." It was going to be a long day.

ALICE

"Alice?" John was hammering on the door. I'd slept far deeper than I'd expected to, the conversation with Lucien had appeased my fear somewhat and sleep came easily. No one had shown up to arrest me for impersonating a student, and if Clarisse had reported me, they would have easily tracked me down by now. The room was in Lucien's name, it would have been simple but so far, nothing. Apart from an increasingly irate John practically banging the door down.

I dragged myself from the warmth of the sheet cocoon I was wrapped up in and walked stiffly across the hotel room. I'd text John the evening before to let him know Lucien was on his way, and I doubted that had made him very happy. Particularly as I was so adamant that we had to finish the job first.

"Morning John," I opened the door, yawning.

John thrust a takeaway coffee at me and barked, "get dressed, quickly."

"Huh?"

"For fuck's sake Alice, don't dawdle, get dressed."

"I need to shower." I said taking the coffee. "Shit, that's hot."

"Alice," he said slowly as though talking to a child, "if you don't get dressed right this minute, I will dress you myself."

"Oh." I said, realisation dawning. "Oh my God, you know where Hettie is?"

John nodded as if I was the dumbest person on the planet.

"I'll get dressed."

"Quickly."

I grabbed the clothes I'd discarded the night before and dressed in the bathroom. I didn't bother to brush my hair, just tied it up in a pony tail and cleaned my teeth as fast as I could before John could get more agitated. He tutted when I stopped to put on my trainers before he guided me out of the room and into a car that had been parked in front of the hotel.

"Where are we going."

"You are the last person to see Isabelle, I want to be sure it's her."

"Shit John, don't give that responsibility to me. What if she sees me."

"There is a disguise on the back seat, put it on."

We didn't speak as John weaved in and out of the morning traffic, one eye on the road and the other on the satnav. All I could hear was the pounding of my heart and feel the intense need to vomit. Had we got close enough? Would Lucien get his wish?

Listlessly I scanned the news pages on my phone. The headlines screamed misery, projections were low, the arse was falling out of the economy and I'd done such little work that the arse would fall out of my business too if I wasn't careful. I had to be more focused, there was no other option if I wanted to stay in business, the award would only get me so far and then I would be on my own.

"We're here." John said. He sent a message on his phone and waited for the reply. "My team are in four locations, now we wait."

"For what?"

"For those gates to open." I looked up at the house facing the street. It was large but not ostentatious, nothing like the chateau that was falling to rack and ruin, but smart and in the most exclusive of areas, befitting of a *brilliant surgeon* – brilliant, lying, murdering, home-wrecker fucktard of a surgeon.

"Oh."

We sat in silence. When I'd imagined a stake out, I had some Hollywood cop film image in my head, but this was nothing like that. There were no wise cracks or baddies in bin lorries, there was nothing. John did a crossword and occasionally checked his phone and I just scanned social media wishing I'd brought my laptop with me. Sitting in a quiet car would have been just the place to get some work done but as it was, I had nothing to do. I was bored. I'd also been up half an hour and I was beginning to feel hungry. The sun was starting to rise, sending pinks and oranges across the sky. It was a beautiful morning, but far too early.

I lay back and closed my eyes. Perhaps I could get another thirty minutes in, but as I began to float, John brought me back to consciousness with a shove from his elbow.

"Is that her?" He asked, turning the engine on. I struggled upright and looked at the car coming along the road. Isabelle was driving and beside her...

183

"Oh, my God, John that's Hettie, I'm sure of it, she looks exactly like Lucien. I swear it's her."

John let the car go a little way before he turned ours around. He pressed a button on his phone and ringing erupted from the speakers.

"John?" A voice said in answer.

"They're heading your way, black Mercedes, two door, two females, follow slowly."

John hung up the phone and dialled another number. "We have them in our sights," he said to the man at the other end. "Jason is following, we're behind. Black merc, two females, careful."

"Will do." The call ended and John phoned the final team member, the same short conversation, the same instructions relayed.

"What do we do now?" I asked John.

"Grace Bissett attends Lady Antoinette's School for Girls in the city, we are making sure she is going there. Then we wait."

"What for?"

John kept a steady pace. "For school to end. Then we drop the bomb."

"The bomb?"

"Lucien."

"You can't do that!" I said aghast. "You can't put him in that situation, John, that's feeding him to the lions, and what about Hettie? You have no idea what she's been led to believe all these years. No, that's all wrong."

"Don't tell me how to do my job, Alice."

"Lucien is coming here with a lawyer and a psychiatrist. We have to get Clarisse out, we have evidence to convict Jean-Claude, that's what we need to do first, before Hettie has her world turned upside down again. Lucien has to decide what to do about Hettie, we just have to know where she is." I searched the school times on my phone. "We have seven hours to get the evidence to the lawyer and onto the police. We have to do that first."

John seemed to relent. "You're in the wrong job," he said after a long pause. "I'm so used to being gung-ho about everything that you're right, I would have played this all wrong. My job has always been to get to Hettie and bugger everything else but you're right, Alice. Absolutely right. We'll do it your way."

184

I felt a surge of relief. "Thank you, John."

He shrugged and slowed the car. "They are going into the school. We'll wait for Isabelle to come out then Jason will follow her. You and I will wait for Lucien, the others can watch the school. One this entrance, one the other entrance and make sure there are no issues." He phoned the team and then we left, turning the car back towards the hotel.

We were so close, I could barely believe it.

LUCIEN

I didn't quite believe what I was hearing. Clarisse, Jean-Claude, Hettie…it was so farfetched that it hardly seemed true, but Alice had laid out all the evidence and I'd listened to the tapes over and over. I struggled to hold back the tears and the relief was shaking my knees until I thought they would buckle. I didn't kill Ottie. It hadn't been me. It was too much to take in that my mind went blank, saving me from the swirling emotions that were rushing through me like a tidal wave.

The blame was laid at Jean-Claude's door. He had lied to me, the sick sonofabitch, stolen my life and left me lying in a hospital bed believing that I had been drunk. What sort of sick fuck did that? He was supposed to have been my best friend, but he had taken a decade of my life and taken everything from Clarisse. Lovely, gentle Clarisse who had been in an institution because she had refused to lie.

I wanted to kill him with my bare hands, squeeze the life from him millimetre by millimetre but that was too good an ending for someone who could sink as low as he had, the prison inmates could take care of him.

The police chief was talking in a hushed voice to Charles and the psychiatrist, Simon, was busy checking European laws on the release of patients. Alice hadn't moved from the chair beside the window, staring out of Zurich with unblinking eyes, a cup of coffee cold beside her. She looked exhausted but she had also never looked more beautiful. I had taken a toll on her, me and my fucked-up life, but she had never wavered, never once made me feel that I was too much. She had saved me, over and over again, bringing me back from the brink each time I thought I would fall.

I didn't ever believe that I would find love again. I'd hidden from it for a decade, the weight of my guilt being a barrier that kept me away from the world. Women were a commodity to use and discard until there was Alice. Beautiful, clever, talented, sexy Alice. She excited my mind, my body and my soul and through her eyes I saw the person I could be, that I wanted to be, and she changed me permanently.

I was in this room because of her. Because she believed in me when I couldn't even believe in myself. Alice never doubted her surety that I didn't kill Ottie, and she had made this happen. We were in touching distance of the finish line, because of her. John admitted to me that he would have made the wrong call and that Alice stopped him before it was too late, and she had been right.

My beautiful Alice. Love of my life. She had saved me once again.

I tuned into the conversation between Charles and the police chief, Fritz.

"I need to take the evidence if I am to convict Mr Benoit." Fritz said, "this is a complicated mess, isn't it?"

"No." I said sharply. "The evidence stays with me, until I have seen Hettie."

"Lucien?" Alice called over, "we have copies, plenty of copies, let him take the originals or the authenticity will be questioned. There cannot be even the faintest chance that Jean-Claude will get away with what he has done, so it's the only way. Trust me, Lucien, a copy won't do. Will he be arrested?" She asked, looking behind me to Fritz.

"Without a doubt, Alice. Although," he said uncomfortably, "there is the small matter of you breaking and entering…"

Alice sighed. "I had a key to the chateau, I told you."

"Yes, well, there is also the matter of falsifying documentation to gain entry into a secure facility."

"That I'll admit to, and if you have to arrest me for that, so be it. If a dying woman gets to go home because I faked my way in, well I can live with the consequences."

"There will be no consequences," Simon said putting his mobile down on the table. "I've just spoken with Stella Zeldig and no charges will be pressed. Dr Zeldig is understandably distraught about Mrs Benoit and she is beyond thankful to Miss Addison for uncovering such a hideous violation of human rights. If anything, Miss Addison is to be commended."

"I don't want a commendation. I just want to know that Clarisse will be looked after."

"I will arrange that," I said fiercely. "She would never have rotted in that place if I'd known…"

"I know, Lucien, she isn't there because of you." She smiled gently at me. "Jean-Claude took everyone down. He'll get his comeuppance."

"He most certainly will," Fritz said, putting on his jacket. "I will be arresting him imminently. Mr Ross, I cannot imagine how you must have felt all these years, believing the very worst of yourself. My condolences for the loss of your daughters at the hands of this man."

"Thank you." I nodded my head. Alice came up beside me and took my hand in hers. I raised her hand to my lips and kissed it, the warm scent of her skin infusing the air around me as I did. She pulled me into her arms, and I relaxed against her, feeling the familiar heart beat behind her breast. "I love you, Alice," I whispered, my lips pressed against her ear. "Thank you."

"Don't thank me yet." She whispered back. "Thank me after you've seen Hettie and Clarisse is where she should be."

"I want to kill him." I said, my arms tensing around Alice's shoulders. She winced and I released her. "I do. I want to tear his limbs off one by one and rip out his heart. He killed Ottie and let me suffer for it. *You were drunk, Lucien. It's a tragic accident, Lucien. You had too much to drink, Lucien. Don't you remember I told you not to drive.* Acid dripped from my tongue as I recalled all the accusatory words that had flowed from him, in the aftermath of Ottie's death, and the great show he'd made of covering things over. He'd run off with my wife and child. He'd killed my daughter and left me in a hospital bed believing it had been my fault.

Cunt.

How I felt about Jean-Claude went so far beyond hate that I almost felt myself tipping into insanity. He'd locked up his wife, had her diagnosed as mentally ill and made up a story to keep her from exposing him as being the murderous sick fuck that he was.

"I want Clarisse out of that place now. Right now. I don't care how you do it," I thundered. Everyone looked up at me shocked. "Simon, Charles, get her out of there now."

188

"Lucien," Alice said gently, her hand on my arm. "Clarisse is very sick, you have to take this slowly."

"Then get a fucking doctor and an ambulance to take her home."

Alice looked at me shaking her head. "She needs more than that, Lucien. She needs to know Jean-Claude has paid the price for what he's done, she needs to know that she's safe."

"She will be, Alice." Fritz said, walking across the room. "Her husband is about to lose his freedom and be sent to prison for a very long time."

Alice looked beseechingly at me. "Do you think I should take her home?" I asked her.

"Not necessarily." She said, "but somehow you have to find someone who will look after her. What about her family? They probably didn't even know where she was, her hospital records were fake. Everything about this whole situation has been fake. There isn't much time, Lucien."

"Get Carol on it. Get John on it, get God on it..." I snapped looking down at my watch. I didn't mean to snap but the time to see Hettie was looming ever closer and I had no idea what I would say or if she would even know me. I felt the weight of the missing years, the empty shell my life had been after my family left. I could remember the grief and guilt and desperate self-hatred that guided me to choices that had been so wrong. I looked over to Alice who'd moved from me, to stand back beside the window. "Sorry." I said.

"I can't imagine how you much be feeling," she said quietly. Simon and Charles looked up from their frantic typing onto laptops to watch us. "I keep trying to put myself in your shoes and to feel what you are feeling but I can't. I don't know how you are processing any of this, to know it wasn't you, after all this time. How do you even begin to accept the lies and deceit? I'm trying to imagine what it would be like if Xander or Anna had done something like this and those feelings, they won't come. I don't know what to say or how to help."

"You just being here helps, Alice. Knowing just how much you've done to get us to this point, helps. Having my back, being my rock, being as sexy as fuck, helps." Alice grinned, Charles and Simon just looked embarrassed. I moved towards her and took her back into my arms, burying my face into her soft neck. "I fucking love you. I fucking love fucking you. I just fucking love being with you. You are the very best thing to ever happen to me and I'm never letting you go. I mean...fuck, Alice, you gave me my life back. All those years my demons chipped away at my soul, it was you who pulled me into the light, every time, and maybe now, because of you, they will leave me in peace."

She didn't say anything, but I felt dampness spread over the shoulder of my shirt. She didn't need to speak because I could feel everything coming from her in waves.

"Lucien?" John said, coming into the room. "It's time to go. Are you ready?"

"Fuck, I don't know..." I let go of Alice and ran across the room to the bathroom where I threw up violently, until my stomach ached, and my throat burned. Was I ready? I didn't fucking know anymore.

LUCIEN

"Jean-Claude has just been arrested on manslaughter charges…" Charles said from his seat in the back of the people carrier.

"Manslaughter? What the fuck? He killed Ottie." My anger took on its own form and Charles shirked back into his seat.

"Don't shoot the messenger, Lucien, and if you'd let me finish, I can also tell you that he's being questioned over Clarisse's sectioning, your poisoning and falsifying medical records. Amongst other things…"

Alice put her hand on my arm to silence me, before she asked, "what does that all exactly mean?"

"It means he will likely have a full life sentence and chances are he'll never be released. If he does, well he will be a very old man. Both of you may have to go to court, especially you Alice, and Clarisse, she may need to testify before time runs out." Charles put his phone into his laptop bag and leaned back in his seat. "He didn't put up a fight, but his lawyer has been called to the police station, so we just have to wait."

"For how long?"

"I don't know, bail could be posted, but equally, bail may be refused because of the severity of the crime and how much media attention it will be attract. Although the case could be brought quickly because Clarisse is so ill. I don't know, I will know when it has all been decided."

"Why will you know?" Alice asked looking from me to Lucien. "Are we in trouble?"

"No, but Lucien is directly involved, it's going to take time."

"What about me?" Alice's voice dipped. "Will I be in trouble?"

I squeezed the hand that was on my arm and she smiled a wobbly smile at me.

"You're not being charged with anything, but you may be questioned and, you have to understand that it could get difficult."

"Difficult how?"

"They could question the validity of your testimony because you got it under false pretences."

"Oh."

191

"Stop scaring her, Charles." I said sharply, "Jean-Claude is the fucking criminal, not Alice."

"It's ok Lucien," Alice said.

"No, it's fucking not…"

"It is!" Alice insisted. "It is all ok. Right now, you need to focus on why we are here, outside this school, and that in a few short minutes you will see Hettie again. Don't start dwelling on things that we can't control, if I get my wrists slapped, then so be it, it would have been worth it – for you, for Clarisse and for your daughters. That's all that matters, a telling off from a judge and being hauled over the coals by a slime bag lawyer, we can handle that when it happens. It's what happens now that counts."

"What if she doesn't want to know…"

"Lucien, my darling Lucien, she will. I know it. She has had pieces missing just as you have…"

Alice was interrupted as a black Mercedes screeched to a halt in front of the school gates. Isabelle got out of the car, forcing the door back so hard on its hinges it slammed shut. She pushed at the intercom on the outside of the school wall and waited, twisting her hair round and round in her hands.

"No, Lucien," Alice said in warning, "don't go now."

The gate beside the panel opened and Isabelle hurried through, leaving the car running in front of the main gates.

"I'm not waiting another moment." I said, opening the car door. Alice looked at John then Charles and back to me. "Don't stop me, Alice. She could be gone before we had the chance to stop her, that's not happening again. No fucking way."

I climbed from the people carrier and ran along the road to the Mercedes. Reaching in, I took the keys from the ignition and threw them into the hedgerow. There was no way I was letting Isabelle out of my sight this time.

ALICE

You could have heard a pin drop in the people carrier. We all sat with breath held as we watched the events unfold in front of us. Lucien had thrown the car keys away and was pacing, like a predator waiting for his prey. Everything that we'd been through had come to this one moment and each one of us in the car was hoping that it would come good.

I prayed to every god I could think of that Hettie would know him. I didn't think my heart would stay in one piece if, after all this time, she rejected him and left with Isabelle. He had searched and searched for her, he had battled the demons that tore him down over and over, to get to this moment. I couldn't feel my arms or my legs, such was my fear for him and if I was feeling like this, how the fuck was he still standing up?

I looked at him – my love. *I'm going to marry you, Alice.* Everything was held in the balance now, our future, his future, my future and Hettie's. What happened next would decide our fate and surely, we all deserved a happy ever after? Lucien did. Ten years of believing the very worst of himself was a punishment that had been completely undeserved. It made me think about love and lust and obsession and what would drive someone to do something as unspeakably hideous as what Jean-Claude had done. Was it fear? Was it to be the alpha male? Was it jealousy or control?

I couldn't get into Jean-Claude's head at all. I loved Lucien with my entire being, but I would never destroy someone else to have him. It was as alien to me as living on Mars. I'd never sleep again if I'd done something like that, it would eat me up until I ended up either mad or dead. I wondered if Jean-Claude's conscience ever woke him up, if the demons that chased Lucien, had also chased him.

Lucien was pacing like a lion in a zoo, back and forth, back and forth, clenching and unclenching his fists, getting paler and paler. I got out of the car, against the protestations of John and Charles, and ran across the road to where Lucien was. Tears were streaming silently down his face and his eyes were haunted with fear. The scar that marred his cheek was an angry red, violent against the grey pallor. I took his hand and paced with him, up and down, very slowly reducing the speed until we were almost standing still.

"What if she tells me to go, Alice." His voice broke and I squeezed his hand tightly. He didn't seem to notice. "What if it's Jean-Claude that she wants, not me, even though he took her sister away? What do I do then?"

"It won't happen, Lucien." I said softly. "You are her dad, Jean-Claude is nothing…"

"He's been her father for ten years."

"No, Lucien, he's not been. He has been there for her, but she's always had a father."

"Fuck Alice, I can't breathe." Lucien gripped his stomach between two hands and bent over. "I can't breathe."

"Lucien, look at me…"

He glanced up and his eyes were hollow.

"Breathe with me, in and out…" I spoke slowly taking deep breathes and blowing them out loudly until his breathing mirrored mine. "That's it, Lucien, big breaths…"

"If people could see me now…" He stood up straight and rubbed his eyes before raking his hands through his hair. "Lucien Ross, wimp."

"Hardly." I remonstrated, "most people would not have gotten through all of this…"

"That's because they don't have you."

I was about to reply when the gate opened, and a pinched-looking Isabelle walked through with a suited man and behind her…

"Hettie!" Lucien yelped causing Isabelle to spin round in horror. Her mouth formed an O and the man beside her didn't react quickly enough before he was forced out of the way by Lucien. "Hettie?" Tears were streaming down his face as he shifted from foot to foot. Henrietta looked scared, her eyes darting to her mother and back again.

"Daddy?" She whispered, "Daddy?"

"Yes, darling girl, yes it's Daddy." Lucien reached out an arm as Hettie took a step backwards.

Isabelle looked as though she were about to faint and the man beside her looked confused. "Hettie?" He asked. Isabelle just nodded and twisted her hands through her hair, over and over like a woman possessed.

"Go away." Hettie screeched, her voice sounding like nails down a blackboard, her face drenched in tears. "Go away and leave me alone. You're not my Daddy. My Daddy wouldn't have left me when Ottie died. Not like you did. My Daddy told me that he would always be there to hold my hand when I was scared, always, but you weren't. Ottie was dead and you left me, like I didn't matter. Like she didn't matter…"

Her face twisted, mirroring the pain on Lucien's face.

"That's not true, Hettie, I was ill…"

"I DON'T CARE. You promised me. I was scared, Daddy, all the time. I was scared that I would be next, that I would die too, like Ottie." Henrietta's face was blurred behind the tears. Lucien's face was deathly grey, and he seemed to shrink in front of my eyes. I moved closer to him but no one else moved. Isabelle looked as though she wanted to speak but the words wouldn't come. Time was standing completely still as we watched two broken people fracture even more.

"I was sick," Lucien coughed a couple of times to heal the break in his voice. "After the accident I was in hospital for months. I would have come for you, Hettie, if I could have. I would never have let you go if I'd been well enough to stop it all."

Hettie's legs shook and her heartbreak seemed to infuse the air around us, clawing at everyone with demonic fingers. "You could have come afterwards. When you were well, but you didn't. You just left me. I wanted you, Daddy, I cried for you all the time, but you never came."

I'd never seen a person more damaged than Lucien before, but Henrietta had also carried the decade on her young shoulders and her life was unravelling before my eyes.

"I could hear Ottie screaming in my head," Hettie said. "It was like she was in the room with me, every single day, and when I was asleep people came to take me, scary people, their faces were hidden with black hoods but I could see their scaly hands, they reached for me but somehow I woke up and they went away. I was too scared to sleep, and Jean-Claude always got cross about it, so I stopped telling

195

him and Mama. Jean-Claude said...he said..." She couldn't go on, instead reached out for the wall to keep her upright.

It was the worst moment of my life. It didn't seem as though the happy ending would come, and I could see Lucien surrendering to the demons that were surrounding him.

"Hettie..." Isabelle moved towards Hettie.

"No. NO." Hettie screamed. "You said Daddy was sick and that was why we had to go. Jean-Claude told me Daddy didn't care about me, that he was a bad man who didn't love me anymore... Jean-Claude said Daddy killed Ottie. And now I don't know what to believe. You are all liars. YOU ALL LIED TO ME."

"I didn't know..." Isabelle whispered looking ill. "I had no idea he said those things to you. I had no idea it was all because of Jean-Claude...because of both of us, I only found out today...This happened because of me. Daddy didn't do anything wrong." Isabelle turned to Lucien with complete desolation on her face. "If I'd known the truth, Lucien..."

"What is the truth?" Hettie interrupted in a strange, flat tone. "What really is the truth? Why didn't Daddy come, why did Jean-Claude kill Ottie, why did everyone lie to me? You told me never to lie yet that is all anyone has ever done. What's the truth?" Her beautiful face crumped. "Someone, anyone, tell me the truth. TELL ME THE TRUTH."

"Hettie?" I said softly, walking towards her and stopping a few feet from where she was. "I'm Alice, Daddy's friend..."

"Friend? Friend or girlfriend." She asked sniffing loudly.

"Girlfriend." I paused for her to have some time then continued, "we have all just found out the truth and everyone is trying to understand it all. I can't imagine how this is making you feel. None of you should have had to go through what you have since Ottie died and her death was the tragic outcome of a bad choice. Your mum believed what Jean-Claude told her, she had no reason not to, he has managed to convince a lot of people that lies were truths and destroyed many lives to hide his guilt. Your mum did what she thought was right, because Jean-Claude told her that it was your Daddy's fault. But whatever lies now need unpicking, the one absolute truth is that Lucien loves you, Hettie, you and Ottie. Not

196

being with you took a part of him away and he has looked for you every, single day. I know, Hettie, I've seen how much he's done to find you…" Henrietta looked from me to Lucien.

"I have looked for you the world over, Hettie." Lucien said, his voice breaking as the emotion became too much. "I have never stopped looking for you. I thought I'd killed Ottie, I thought I'd lost both my girls because of what I did. Your mum had to protect you, like Alice said, she did the right thing because she didn't know the truth, but I promise, I have searched for you, Hettie. I am here because we finally got the truth…We found you…I didn't think this day would ever come."

"Daddy." Hettie could barely get the word out. Isabelle was holding onto the man, who I assumed was the head teacher, with both hands gripped around his forearm. She looked close to collapse. "Did you really look for me?"

"Every single day."

"Really?"

"Yes, darling girl, I didn't stop looking for you."

Hettie paused and no one said anything. She seemed to be trying to process everything, to make sense of the chaos her life had just become. I couldn't imagine what it must have been like to have everything you'd been led to believe, turn out to be a lie. I even felt sorry for Isabelle, to have to now carry the burden of Ottie's death being, in part, due to her but mostly because of the man she had chosen to love. I wouldn't have wished Lucien's demons on anyone, but I could see them standing beside Isabelle, ready to pounce. It couldn't happen. Those demons couldn't have another soul. They'd already taken too much.

"I missed you, Daddy. I missed you so much. I talked to you every night before I went to sleep just in case you heard me." She said, wiping her eyes on her school blazer. "Jean-Claude looked after me, he gave me things, but it never felt right without you. I felt so guilty because I wanted you, not him, that I tried to make it right, so that Mummy would be happy, but she was always sad. It was hard not to believe what Jean-Claude told me, and he was nasty to me if I ever mentioned you or Ottie. I had a photo of you and her under my bed, but he found it and took it away. We were only

197

allowed one photo of Ottie up, in Mama's dressing room, where he couldn't see it. He said it was because it made him feel sad...I suppose it was guilt, he was guilty, because he killed her. He said you did it..." Hettie choked on a sob, "it was what I had to believe. That you did it. I didn't want to believe it, but Jean-Claude told me over and over...I waited for you Daddy. I used to send you invitations to my birthday parties when I was small. I put them in the post when Mama or Jean-Claude weren't looking...you never came, and I was always so sad. I wanted you there so much and I thought you didn't come because you didn't love me anymore. I only stopped sending them last year..." She smiled so sadly my heart splintered.

"Hettie..."

"Did you miss me?" She sounded like a small child looking for reassurance.

"Did I miss you? Oh God, Hettie, I missed you every moment of every single day. You and Ottie. I almost gave up hope and then Alice..." He turned to me and smiled. "Alice gave me hope that I would find you, it's because of her that I did. I love you Hettie, I love you so much, I've always loved you, my beautiful baby girl. I'll never let go of your hand again. Ever."

Lucien's face crumpled and he reached his hand out to her. This time, she didn't move away, but put her small hand inside of his and allowed herself to be enveloped in his arms. They clung to one another, sobbing and for me, the world disappeared under my own tears. We had made it. They were free.

The demons had stopped talking.

EPILOGUE

It had been a beautiful New Years' Eve wedding. Despite Xander's worries that the nineteen-eighties were making a comeback, both his and Hugo's mothers had created the perfect wedding. There hadn't been a dry eye in the grand drawing room when Hugo and Xander had exchanged their vows and as the evening drew to a close, the ballroom still lit up with their happiness.

"What are you wishing for the new year?" Lucien asked wrapping his arms around me as we watched the couples swaying out of time to the ballads.

"No drama!" I laughed. "Peace, harmony and a drama free year."

"Do you know what I'm wishing for?"

"I can only imagine!"

"Hey!" Lucien feigned hurt then grinned. "Yeah, lots of that, but there is something else…"

"Oh?"

"Yeah." He leaned his head on my shoulder and pulled me back closer to him. "I'd never have gotten through this year without you, Alice Addison. I owe you everything I have for saving me, for giving me back my daughter."

Hettie and Isabelle had moved to London after Jean-Claude's trial. It had been a long and very difficult time in court with Lucien having to relive painful moments over and over until the Judge, and the lawyers were satisfied. Clarisse's testimony had been given over video link as she was too sick to travel, but there was no doubting her story and the jury took only a few hours to decide on Jean-Claude's guilt.

Afterwards, Lucien and Hettie went backpacking through South America, getting to know each other and making memories that could finally push away the sadness. When they returned, Isabelle had made a new home for her and Hettie in London, not too far from Lucien's apartment, and a calmness had settled over our lives.

Hettie and I had become the best of friends and although Isabelle and my relationship would never be strong, we could be comfortable around each other and it just made things so much better. I was really happy. It scared me to be so happy, but I went with it. The only sadness that touched us was the passing of Clarisse, but she died surrounded by the family who had lost her all those years before. I'm told she was smiling as she took her final breath.

"You really are my guardian angel," Lucien said as the wedding guests began the new year count down. He kissed me softly as the fireworks banged above us. "Happy New Year."

"Happy New Year, Lucien, may it be the best one yet." I grinned. "Just more peaceful, and calm…"

"Now, that's the problem," he said smiling at me, "I've been thinking all day how beautiful you'd look in ivory…"

"Ivory?"

"I told you I was going to marry you Alice Addison," Lucien knelt down in front of me as the cheers of New Year rang out around us. "And I intend to do just that."

"You do?" I squeaked as Lucien took a small box from his pocket. He opened it and a large diamond glittered under the fairy lights.

"Marry me?" He asked slipping the ring onto my finger. "Marry me, Alice."

I knelt down and, wrapping my arms around Lucien, I kissed him. It was a kiss of a thousand tomorrows, of promises and dreams and a bright future.

"Yes," I whispered against his lips. "Yes, I'll marry you."

"About fucking time!" Xander said, picking my hand up from Lucien's shoulder, "now get up you lovebirds, we're dancing."

And we did, all night…well, you know, almost all night, there were plenty of ways to welcome in a new year, and with Lucien, the list of ways was endless!

THE END

Author's Note

Thank you so much for reading my book. I hope you enjoyed the final chapter in the story, particularly now that Alice and Lucien have found their 'happy-ever-after' (despite the uncertainty in Red and Blush)!

I'm always bereft when I've typed *The End*, and in the case of Alice and Lucien, it's felt more emotional than normal because I didn't expect to write three books. When I started Red, it was supposed to be a stand-alone, yet here I am, three books later, with no more story to tell. Yep, I've shed a few tears about that! Still, they're happy, I'm happy, so that's it for Alice and Lucien, they go on without me!

Onto the next story...!!

E: katienewmanauthor@outlook.com
F: Katie Jane Newman
I: @katiejanenewmanwriter
T: @KJNewmanAuthor
W:www.katiejanenewman.co.uk

Thank You

Amanda, Beth, Cinzia, Gill, Leah and Nicola
My EPIC test readers xxx

Finally,
Mistakes? All mine, sorry!

Printed in Great Britain
by Amazon